THE WAVES EXTINGUISH THE WIND

THE

WAVES

EXTINGUISH

THE WIND

ARKADY & BORIS STRUGATSKY

A NEW TRANSLATION BY
DANIELS UMANOVSKIS

CHICAGO
REVIEW
PRESS

Published by Chicago Review Press Incorporated
814 North Franklin Street
Chicago, IL 60610
ISBN 978-1-64160-626-4

Library of Congress Control Number: 2023930804

Cover design: Jonathan Hahn
Cover photo: Danny Iacob / Shutterstock

Typesetting: Nord Compo

Printed in the United States of America

To understand is to simplify.

—D. Strogov

INTRODUCTION

My name is Maxim Kammerer. I am eighty-nine.

Once upon a time I read an ancient novella that begins in such a manner. I remember thinking then that, should I ever write a memoir, I would begin similarly. However, this text cannot strictly be considered a memoir, and it should begin with a letter I received about a year ago:

> Kammerer,
> You have surely read the notorious *Five Biographies of Our Age*. Please help me identify who is hiding behind the pseudonyms P. Soroka and E. Brown. You will, I assume, find it easier than I do.
> *M. Glumova*
> *June 13 '225, Novgorod*

I never replied to this letter, because I didn't manage to discover the real names of the authors of *Five Biographies of Our Age*. I could only establish that, as expected, P. Soroka and E. Brown were prominent members of the Ludens Group at the Institute for Space History Studies (ISHS).

I could easily imagine what Maya Toivovna Glumova felt as she read her son's biography as presented by P. Soroka and E. Brown. And I realized that I had to say my part.

I wrote this memoir.

To a nonprejudiced and, in particular, a young reader, this memoir will address events that ended an entire era of humanity's cosmological self-perception and, it seemed at first, opened up new possibilities that had previously been considered only in theory. I was a witness to and participant in these events, to some degree even their initiator, so it is unsurprising that the Ludens Group has been bombarding me for years with the relevant requests, with official and unofficial solicitations of assistance and reminders of my civic duty. I had initially been understanding and sympathetic toward the group's goals, but I also never hid my skepticism regarding their chances of success. Moreover, it was entirely clear to me that the materials and information I personally possess cannot be of any use to the Ludens Group, and therefore I have until now avoided any participation in their work.

But now, due to reasons mostly of a private nature, I felt compelled after all to collect and offer to anyone interested everything I know about the first days of the Great Revelation, about the events that essentially were the reason for that storm of discussions, fears, concerns, disagreements, protestations, and above all the incredible surprise—everything that is usually called the Great Revelation.

Rereading that previous paragraph, I have to correct myself. First, I am of course not offering nearly all that I know. Some materials are too sensitive to present here. I will omit some names due to purely ethical considerations. I'll also refrain from mentioning some particular methods of my work at that time as the director of the Department of Unconventional Events (UE) in the Commission for Control (COMCON-2).

Second, the events of '99 were, strictly speaking, not the first days of the Great Revelation but, on the contrary, its last days. That is exactly why it, the Great Revelation, is by now merely a subject for historical studies. And this is exactly what the Ludens Group doesn't understand—or, more precisely, isn't willing to accept, despite all my efforts to be convincing. Perhaps I haven't been insistent enough. I've grown old.

The personality of Toivo Glumov, naturally, attracts particular, I would even say special, attention from members of the Ludens Group. I understand them and have therefore made him a central figure in this memoir.

Of course, that isn't the only or even the main reason. Regardless of why I reminiscence about those days, and no matter what I remember, Toivo Glumov is the first image in my mind—I see his lean, always serious young face, with his long white eyelashes always low over his clear gray eyes; I hear his voice, seeming deliberately slow; I sense his silent pressure, helpless but relentless like a silent scream: *Well, what is it? Why are you not acting? Order me!* And, conversely, as soon as I remember him for any reason, the angry hounds of my memory awaken as if from a rough kick—all the horror of those days, all the desperation of those days, all the helplessness of those days. Horror, desperation, and helplessness that I went through alone, because I had nobody to share them with.

Documents are the foundation of the present memoir. These are mostly standard form reports from my inspectors, as well as some official letters that I am including mainly in an attempt to reproduce the atmosphere of those days. A nitpicky and competent researcher would easily notice that a number of relevant documents are not included, while some of the included ones don't seem necessary. I'll address this criticism right away by saying that I selected the materials according to certain criteria that I have no particular desire or need to expand upon.

Further, a significant part of the text consists of reconstructed chapters. They are written by me personally and reconstruct scenes and events that I was not witness to. The reconstructions are based on testimony, recordings, and later recollections of the people involved in said events, among them Toivo Glumov's wife Asya, his colleagues, acquaintances, etc. I realize that those chapters are of little value to members of the Ludens Group, but be it as it may, they're very valuable to me.

Finally, I took the liberty of interspersing this text with my own reminiscences, which are not so much about contemporary events as they are about the fifty-eight-year-old Maxim Kammerer. This man's behavior under the given circumstances seems interesting to me even now, thirty-one year later.

Having made the decision to write this memoir, I arrived at the question: Where do I begin? When and how did the Great Revelation begin?

Strictly speaking, it all began two centuries ago, with the sudden discovery deep beneath the Martian surface of an empty tunneled city built out of amberine. That is when the word "Wanderers" was first spoken. That is true. But too general. You could just as well say that the Great Revelation began with the Big Bang.

Maybe fifty years ago, then? The "foundlings case"? When the problem of the Wanderers first took on a tragic undertone, and when the reproachful barb "Sikorsky syndrome" was born and spread by word of mouth? An uncontrollable fear of a possible Wanderer invasion? True as well, and much more to the point . . . but I was not director of the Department of Unconventional Events then; the department didn't even exist at the time. And I am not writing a history of the Wanderers issue here.

For me, it started in May '93, when I, like all other UE directors of all COMCON-2 sectors, received a brief about an incident on Tisza (not the river calmly going through Hungary and Transcarpathia, but the planet Tisza orbiting EN 63061, recently discovered by the FSG fellows). The memo presented the incident as a case of sudden unexplainable insanity of all three members of an exploration party that had landed on a plateau (I forgot the name) two weeks earlier. All three suddenly became convinced that they had lost communications with the base, lost all communications with everyone except the orbiting mothership, and this mothership was repeating an automatic broadcast saying the Earth had been destroyed in some cosmic cataclysm, and all the population of the Periphery had died of some mysterious epidemic.

I don't remember all the details anymore. Two of the party, I think, tried to commit suicide and ended up going into the desert, desperate beyond themselves with the hopelessness and pointlessness of future existence. The party's commander, however, turned out to be a hard man. He forced himself to live through gritted teeth, as if not all humanity had died but rather he himself had fallen victim to an accident that forever cut him off from his planet. Later he said that, on the fourteenth day of this mad existence, some figure in white appeared and announced that he, the commander, had honorably passed the first trial and become a candidate for joining the Wanderer society. On the fifteenth day, an emergency bot arrived from the mothership and things returned to normal. Those gone to the desert were found, everyone was in their right mind, nobody got harmed. Their testimonies matched to the minute details. For example, they all identically reproduced the accent heard in the supposed emergency broadcast. Subjectively, they experienced the events as a vivid, incredibly believable stage play in which they had become actors against their will and expectations. A deep mentoscopy confirmed this subjective feeling and even showed that, at the deepest subconscious levels, they had all been sure that the whole thing was just theatrics.

As far as I know, my colleagues in other sectors took the memo as a fairly ordinary unconventional event, an unexplained case the likes of which are common on the Periphery. Everyone's alive and healthy. No additional work in the vicinity of the UE is necessary, or was ever necessary. Nobody is interested in diving into the mystery. The UE's area was evacuated. The UE was duly noted. Off to the archives.

But I was a student of the late Sikorsky! When he was alive, I had often argued with him—both mentally and openly—when it came to external threats to humanity. Still, I couldn't argue with one argument of his, nor did I want to: "We work at COMCON-2. We can afford to be known as ignorant, superstitious mystics. The one thing we cannot afford is to underestimate a threat. And if our house suddenly smells of sulfur, it is our obligation to assume that Lucifer himself has turned up nearby and to take the appropriate measures, up to and including organizing the production of holy water on an industrial scale." And as soon as I got word of someone in white speaking on behalf of the Wanderers, I smelled sulfur and roused myself like an old warhorse at the sound of a trumpet.

I made appropriate inquiries using the appropriate channels. I was not particularly surprised to discover that the vocabulary of our COMCON-2 instructions, orders, and plans doesn't contain the word "Wanderer." I was in meetings with the highest echelons of our hierarchy and was then completely unsurprised to see that, as far as our most responsible leaders were concerned, the issue of Wanderer progressor activities within human society is no more. Passed like a childhood illness. It was as if the tragedy of Lev Abalkin and Rudolf Sikorsky somehow inexplicably removed all suspicion from the Wanderers, now and forever.

The only person to display a measure of sympathy for my concerns was Athos-Sidorov, the president of my sector and my direct superior. Under his authority he approved and with his signature he confirmed the subject I proposed, "The Visit of the Old Lady." He allowed me to organize a special group to work the subject. Actually, he gave me full discretion on the issue.

I began by arranging an expert survey among the most competent specialists in xenosociology. My goal was to create a model (the most likely one) of Wanderer progressor activity within the human society on Earth. Without delving into details, I sent all my materials to the renowned historian of science and erudite Isaac Bromberg. I don't even remember why I did it; Bromberg had been away from xenology for many years by then. I suppose it was because most specialists whom I asked my questions to simply refused to seriously discuss the matter with me (Sikorsky syndrome!), but Bromberg was known to "always have a few words up his sleeve," no matter the subject.

Anyhow, Dr. I. Bromberg sent me his response, which is now known to specialists as the "Bromberg memorandum."

Everything began with it.

I will begin with it as well.

(END OF INTRODUCTION)

DOCUMENT 1

To: COMCON-2
    Ural-North Sector
    Maxim Kammerer
    To be handed personally. Official business.
Date: June 3, '94
Author: I. Bromberg, senior consultant of COMCON-1, doctor
    of historical sciences, laureate of the Herodotus Prize '63,
    '69 & '72, professor, laureate of the John Amos Comenius
    Minor Prize '57, doctor of xenopsychology, doctor of socio-
    topology, full member of the Academy of Sociology (Europa),
    corresponding member of the Laboratorium (Academy of
    Sciences) of Great Tagora, magister of Parseval abstraction
    realization
Subject: 009, "The Visit of the Old Lady"
Contents: A working model of Wanderer progressor activities
    among the people of Earth

Dear Kammerer!

Please do not consider the pompously official header of this message to be some old man's mockery. I just wanted to underscore that my message, while quite private, is at the same time entirely official. I remember the header of your own reports from the time when our poor Sikorsky threw them onto my desk as some kind of (pretty pathetic) argument.

My attitude toward your organization has not changed a bit; I have never hidden it and you are definitely well aware of it. The materials that you sent me I studied, however, with great interest. I thank you. I would like to assure you that, in this line of your work (and only this one!), I am your most devoted ally and colleague.

I don't know if it was a coincidence, but your "Summary of Models" arrived just as I was planning to begin summarizing my own many years of thought concerning the nature of the Wanderers, and their inevitable collision with Earth's civilization. I am, however, of the firm conviction that coincidences do not exist. It would seem that the time has come for this.

I have neither the time nor the inclination to offer a detailed criticism of your document. I cannot fail to remark that the "Octopus" and "Conquistador" models brought on a fit of uncontrollable laughter by being such primitive jokes, while the "New Air" model appears to be a nontrivial construction but is utterly devoid of any serious arguments. Eight models! Eighteen creators, among them such stars as Karibanov, Yasuda, Mikich! Dammit, something more worthwhile could have been expected! See it as you wish, Kammerer, but naturally the assumption arises that you failed to impress upon these grandmasters your "concerns about our general unpreparedness on this issue." They just wrote to be rid of you.

Hereby I humbly bring to the pedestal of your attention a brief annotation of my upcoming book, which I plan to title *Monocosm: The Pinnacle or the First Step? Notes on the Evolution of Evolution.* Once again I lack the time and inclination to provide any level of detailed argumentation for my basic statements. I can only assure you that, even today, each of those statements could be supported by exhaustive arguments, so I will be happy to answer any questions that you may have. (By the way, I cannot refrain from noting that your request for my consultation might be the first, and so far only, socially beneficial action taken by your organization in its entire history.)

So: the Monocosm.

Any Intelligence—technological, Rousseauist, or even gerontocratic—undergoes a first-order evolutionary process from the state of maximum disunity (savagery, mutual aggression, limited emotions, mistrust) to the state of maximum unity that still preserves individuality (friendliness, highly developed relationship culture, altruism, a disregard for personal achievement). This process is guided by biological laws, as well as biosocial and specific social ones. It is well studied and is only of interest here because it leads to the question: What next? Leaving aside the romantic trills of vertical progress theory, we discover that Intelligence has only two real and radically different possibilities. One is coming to a halt, self-pacifying, looking inward with a loss of interest in the physical world. The other is stepping onto the path of second-order evolution, the path of controlled and planned evolution, the path toward Monocosm.

The synthesis of Intelligences is inevitable. It offers uncountable new ways to perceive the world, which leads to the unfathomable increase in the amount and, more important, quality of information that can be consumed, which in turn leads to the decrease of suffering to a minimum and the increase of happiness to a maximum. The concept of "home" takes on a universal scale. (This is probably why this irresponsible and superficial term *Wanderers* became colloquial.) A new metabolism emerges and, as a consequence, a healthy life stretches on to practically infinity. An individual's age becomes comparable to that of astronomical bodies, and that's with no accumulation of mental exhaustion. A Monocosm individual has no need for creators. He is a creator and consumer of culture. From a drop of water, he can re-create not only the ocean but also the entire world and its population, including intelligent creatures. And all of this while experiencing a constant, unquenchable sensory hunger.

Each new individual appears as a work of syncretic art, being created by physiologists, geneticists, engineers, psychologists, aestheticians, teachers, and philosophers of the Monocosm. The process, undoubtedly, takes several Earth decades and is, of course, a most exciting and respected line of work for the Wanderers. Modern humanity knows of no analogues to such art, with the possible exception of the rare few cases of Great Love.

Create without destroying—that is the Monocosm's motto.

The Monocosm necessarily considers its development path and its modus vivendi as the only right one. It feels pain and desperation when seeing disunited Intelligences that are not yet ready to join it. It is forced to wait while the Intelligence, in its first-order evolution, develops into a planetary-level society. Only after that can interference into the biological structure begin with the goal of preparing the bearers of Intelligence for joining this monocosmic organism of the Wanderers. No good can come out of Wanderer interference in the fates of disunited civilizations.

A meaningful consideration: the progressors from Earth are ultimately trying to accelerate the creation of more perfect social structures among suffering civilizations. Thus they are also preparing new material for the Monocosm to eventually work with.

We now know of three civilizations that consider themselves prosperous.

Leonidans. A very ancient civilization (no less than three hundred thousand years old, no matter what the late Park Jin might have said). They are the example of a "slow" civilization; they are frozen in unity with nature.

Tagorans. A civilization of hyperdeveloped prudence. Three-quarters of their efforts are spent on examining the negative consequences that could arise from a discovery, an invention, a new technological process, and so on. This civilization appears strange to us only because we cannot understand how interesting it is to prevent negative outcomes, what a massive intellectual and emotional pleasure it is. Slowing progress is as exciting as creating it—depending on one's starting point and upbringing. As a result, they only have public transportation, no aviation at all, but extremely advanced communications technology.

The third civilization is ours, and now we understand why the Wanderers have to interfere with our lives first and foremost. We're *in movement*. We're in movement and therefore we may choose the direction incorrectly.

Nobody even remembers the "prodderpushers" who tried, with fantastic enthusiasm, to force progress onto Tagorans and

Leonidans. Everyone understands by now that trying to prod and push such civilizations, perfect in their own way, is as useless and hopeless as trying to make a tree, an oak for instance, grow faster by pulling its branches up. The Wanderers are no "prodderpushers"; they do not and cannot have the goal of forcing progress. Their goal is the identification, preparation, and, ultimately, introduction into the Monocosm of individuals that are ready for it. I do not know what principles the Wanderers employ in this sorting, and that is unfortunate, for whether we want it or not, if we're frank, without circumlocution or sciencey jargon, here's what it comes down to.

First: humanity's entry into the second order of evolution practically means the transformation of *Homo sapiens* into Wanderer.

Second: most likely, far from all *Homo sapiens* are suitable for this transformation.

To summarize:

- humanity will be split into two unequal parts
- humanity will be split into two unequal parts by some criteria unknown to us
- humanity will be split into two unequal parts by some criteria unknown to us, and the smaller part will forcefully and irreversibly surpass the greater part
- humanity will be split into two unequal parts by some criteria unknown to us, the smaller part will forcefully and irreversibly surpass the greater part, and all of this will come to pass through the will and art of a supercivilization decidedly alien to humanity

Dear Kammerer! As a sociopsychological exercise, I submit to your analysis the situation described above, which is not devoid of novelty.

Now that you somewhat understand the essentials of the Monocosm's progressor strategy, you are likely better equipped than I am to identify the main counterstrategies and the tactics to uncover elements of Wanderer action. It is clear that their search for and preparation of individuals ready for the merger has to be accompanied by circumstances and events that would not elude a careful observer. For example, the appearance of mass phobias, new messianic teachings, the appearance of people with unusual abilities, inexplicable disappearances of people, sudden magic-like acquisition of new talents by some people are some of the things that can be expected. I would also highly recommend that you keep a close eye on the Tagorans and bigheads accredited on Earth—their sensitivity toward the foreign and the unknown is much higher than ours. (In this vein, it is also prudent to monitor the behavior of Earth animals, particularly herd animals with vestiges of intelligence.)

Naturally, your sphere of interest should not be limited to Earth but should include the solar system as a whole, the Periphery and particularly the young Periphery.

Wishing you success,

Yours,

I. Bromberg

(END OF DOCUMENT 1)

DOCUMENT 2

To: President of Ural-North Sector
Date: June 13, '94
Author: M. Kammerer, director of UE Department
Subject: 009, "The Visit of the Old Lady"
Contents: Death of I. Bromberg

President,
Professor Isaac Bromberg suddenly passed away on the morning of June 11, at the Bezhin Meadow Sanatorium.

No notes regarding the "Monocosm" model nor any notes whatsoever regarding the Wanderers have been found in his personal archives. We're continuing to search.

See the attached coroner's report.

M. Kammerer

(END OF DOCUMENT 2)

✦✦✦

This is the exact order in which my young trainee Toivo Glumov read the documents in early '95, and of course the documents made a certain impression on him and necessarily gave him quite specific assumptions, which also fit the grimmest of his expectations. The seed had fallen on good soil. He immediately found the coroner's report and, having discovered exactly nothing in it to confirm his seemingly natural suspicions, requested permission to meet with me.

I remember that morning well: gray, snowy, with a real blizzard outside my office windows. I remember it so well perhaps because of the contrast, as my body was here, in the wintery

Urals, and my eyes were absently following the drops of melting snow on the glass, but in my mind I was looking at a tropical night above the warm ocean, with a naked dead body swaying on the phosphorescent foam, carried by the tides to a gentle, sandy beach. I had just received information from Central about the third death on Matuku Island.

At that moment Toivo Glumov appeared in front of me, and I dispelled my imagination as I asked him to sit and speak. With no introductions, he asked me whether the investigation into Dr. Bromberg's death had been concluded.

I responded, with a measure of surprise, that there wasn't any investigation, just like there wasn't anything special about the death of a century-and-a-half-old man.

Where, in that case, were Dr. Bromberg's notes on the Monocosm?

I explained that such notes, presumably, never existed. Dr. Bromberg's letter was in all likelihood an improvisation. Dr. Bromberg was brilliant at improvisation.

Should that be taken to mean, then, that Dr. Bromberg's letter and the notification of his death that Maxim Kammerer sent to the president happened to be next to one another by coincidence?

I looked at him, at his thin lips pursed in determination, at white hair falling over his low brow, and it was perfectly clear to me what he wanted to hear. *Yes, Toivo my boy*, he would have liked to hear. *I am thinking the same. Bromberg was on to something; the Wanderers got rid of him and stole his priceless papers.* But I was not, of course, thinking any of that, and I did not tell my boy Toivo anything like that. Why the two documents had been next to one another I did not know. Probably a coincidence indeed. That was my explanation to him.

Then he asked me if Bromberg's ideas were being developed in practice.

I responded that the issue was under consideration. All eight models that the experts proposed had quite a lot to criticize. As for Bromberg's ideas, the circumstances were not conductive to treating them seriously.

Then he gathered the courage to ask me directly whether I, Director Maxim Kammerer, was going to develop Bromberg's ideas. This was my opportunity to finally make him happy. He got to hear exactly what he wanted to hear.

"Yes, my boy," I said. "That is why I took you into my department."

He left happy. Neither of us suspected, of course, that he had just taken his first step toward the Great Revelation.

I'm a practical psychologist. When speaking to someone, leaving false modesty aside, I am able to constantly feel the person's emotional state, the direction of their thoughts, and to predict their actions quite well. But if someone asked me to explain how I do that or, worse yet, asked me to draw or put into words the images in my mind, I would find myself in a difficult situation. Like any practical psychologist, I would be forced to resort to analogies from art and literature. I'd refer to Shakespeare, or Dostoyevsky, or Strogov, or Michelangelo, or Johann Surd.

Well, then Toivo Glumov reminded me of the Mexican, Rivera. I mean from the classic Jack London story. Twentieth century. Or the nineteenth, I don't remember exactly.

Toivo Glumov was a progressor by training. Specialists told me that he could have become a progressor of the highest class, an ace progressor. He had outstanding skills. He was excellent at self-control, possessed an exceptionally calm mind and lightning-quick reflexes, and he was a natural at acting and impersonation. And so, after a little over three years of work as a progressor, he resigned for no clear reason and returned to Earth. Right after his reconditioning, he checked the GWI and had no difficulty discovering that the only organization on the planet possibly related to his new goals was COMCON-2.

He appeared in front of me in December '94, full of steely determination to answer questions, again and again, about why he, such a promising, perfectly healthy, highly rewarded progressor suddenly abandons his work, his comrades, ruining meticulous plans and extinguishing the high hopes many had for him . . . of course, I asked nothing of the kind. I didn't care at all why he no longer wanted to be a progressor. I wanted to know why he suddenly wanted to become a counter-progressor of sorts.

His reply was memorable. He disliked the very idea of progressors. He would prefer not to go into detail. It's just that he, a progressor, is conceptually against progressor activity. And back there (he indicated behind his shoulder with a thumb) he had a trivial thought: while he was shaking his codpiece and brandishing his sword, trampling the cobblestones squares of Arkanar, over here (he pointed to the ground with his index finger) some swindler in a fashionable rainbow overcoat would be strolling through the squares of Sverdlovsk, metavisor slung over his shoulder. As far as he, Toivo Glumov, knows, this simple idea comes to few minds, and if it does then it is in a romantic or comedic way. But he, Toivo Glumov, is haunted by the same idea. No gods may be allowed to interfere in our affairs, gods have no business here on Earth, because "the wind is a gift from gods; it fills the sails, but also births storms." (It was difficult to track the quote down later—turns out, it's from Verbliben.)

I could see with my naked eye that I was faced with a fanatic. Unfortunately, as any fanatic, he was prone to extremes of judgment. (Take for instance his statements on progressors, which I will bring up later.) A Catholic far more devout than the pope—me, that is. But he was ready to act. And with no further discussion, I took him on and assigned him to "The Visit of the Old Lady."

He turned out to be an excellent worker. He had energy, he had initiative, he was tireless. And—a very rare quality at his age—he was not discouraged by setbacks. Negative outcomes did not exist for him. More than that, he was as encouraged by negative outcomes of investigations as he was by the rare positive ones. It was as if he had initially assumed that nothing specific would be found in his lifetime, and so he could derive pleasure from the (often rather mundane) work of analyzing any unconventional event that was in the least suspicious. It was great to see my old employees—Grisha Serosovin, Sandro Mtbevari, Andrei Kikin, and others—step up their efforts in his company, stop slacking off, become much less ironic and more professional. And it wasn't a matter of them following Toivo's lead—that was out of the question, he was too young and too green for them—it was as if his seriousness and concentration on the work was contagious. But most of all, I think they were amazed by his deep hatred toward the object of their work, a feeling visible in him that the others totally lacked. I once mentioned the dusky young Rivera in passing to Grisha Serosovin and soon found out that they had all found and read the story by Jack London.

Just like Rivera, Toivo had no friends. He was surrounded by trusted and reliable colleagues, and he was a trusted and reliable partner in anything, but he never acquired any friends. I suppose it was too difficult to be his friend—he was never happy with himself in any area, and so he never went easy on anyone else. He had this kind of merciless concentration on his goal, the sort of which I had only seen in top athletes and scientists. Hardly any place for friendship there . . .

Although he did have one friend. I mean his wife, Asya Stasova, or Anastasia Pavlovna. When I first met her, she was a wonderful small woman, lively as quicksilver, with a witty tongue and highly prone to audacious thoughts and rash decisions, so the atmosphere in their home was always nearly that of a battlefield, and it was a pleasure to observe (from the outside only) their constant verbal clashes.

It was particularly wondrous to behold since usually, at work that is, Toivo seemed to be a rather slow man of few words. He seemed to be constantly slowed down by some important idea preoccupying his mind. But not with Asya. Never with Asya! With her, he was Demosthenes, Cicero, St. Paul: he prophesized, he coined aphorisms, damn, he even ironized! It was hard to even imagine how different those two people were, the slow and silent

Toivo Glumov at Work and the lively, talkative Toivo Glumov at Home, talking philosophy, constantly committing fallacies and passionately defending the same. At home he even enjoyed eating. Even complained about the food. Asya was a gastronomist and taster, and always cooked herself. That was the tradition in her mother's house and her grandmother's house. This tradition that so excited Toivo Glumov went back centuries in the Stasov family, to the unimaginable times before molecular cooking, when a simple meat patty had to be prepared with many complicated and unappetizing steps.

Toivo also had a mother. Every day, no matter where he was or what he was occupied with, he would find a minute to call her on the video channel and at least exchange a few words. They called it the check-in call. Many years ago I had met Maya Toivovna Glumova, but the circumstances of our meeting were so tragic that we never met again. Through no fault of mine. Through no fault of anyone, actually. To put it briefly, she did not hold me in high regard, and Toivo knew that. He never mentioned her to me. But he talked about me a lot with her—something I found out much later.

This bifurcation doubtlessly annoyed Toivo and weighed on him. I don't think Maya Toivovna spoke ill of me to him. And it is unimaginable that she would have told her son the horrible story of Lev Abalkin's death. Most likely, whenever Toivo spoke of his direct superior, she coldly evaded the subject. But even that was more than enough.

I was, after all, more than a superior to Toivo. I was essentially his only like-minded associate, the only person in the giant entirety of COMCON-2 that treated the ideas Toivo was consumed by seriously, with no ifs and buts. He also treated me with great deference. After all, his superior was the legendary Mak Sim! Toivo had not even been born yet when Mak Sim was on Saraksh, blowing up radiation towers, fighting fascists . . . The unequaled White Ferz! The organizer of Operation Virus, after which the superpresident himself gave him the nickname

Big Bug! Toivo was a schoolboy when Big Bug infiltrated the Island Empire, their capital—the first from Earth to do so, and the last . . . Of course, all these were the feats of a progressor, but it is said that a progressor can only be defeated by a progressor! A simple idea that Toivo fervently subscribed to.

And then there's this. Toivo had no idea what to do if Wanderer interference in Earth matters were proven beyond any doubt. There were no comparisons to be drawn from the centuries of human progressor activity. To the Duke of Irukan, an unmasked progressor from Earth was a demon or a practicing sorcerer. To the counterintelligence of the Island Empire, the same progressor was a cunning spy from the continent. But what is a Wanderer progressor to a COMCON-2 agent?

A captured sorcerer was to be burned; it would also do to just throw him into an oubliette and force him to turn his own shit into gold. A spy from the continent was to be turned or eliminated. What to do, then, with an unmasked Wanderer?

Toivo had no answers to such questions. None of his associates had answers to such questions. Most didn't even consider the questions to be meaningful. "What if a merman's beard gets caught in the engine of your boat? Untangle it, cut it? Grab the merman by his face?" Toivo never discussed the subject with me. He never did because, I think, he had already convinced himself that Big Bug, the legendary White Ferz, the cunning Mak Sim, had long since thought it all through, analyzed all the possibilities, prepared detailed plans, and gotten them approved at the highest levels.

I did not disappoint him. For a while at least. I have to say, Toivo Glumov was a man of prejudices (how could he not be, with his fanaticism?). For example, he steadfastly refused to admit a connection between his subject "The Visit of the Old Lady" and another subject we had worked on for a while, "Rip Van Winkle." Cases of sudden and completely inexplicable disappearances of people in the '70s and '80s, and their equally sudden and inexplicable reappearances, were the only part of the Bromberg memorandum that Toivo adamantly refused to consider at all. "What he wrote here is wrong," he would say, "or we have misunderstood something. Why would the Wanderers need people to vanish with no explanation?" And that's despite the Bromberg memorandum having become his catechism, a plan for his life's entire work . . . Apparently he couldn't, didn't want to contend with the Wanderers having almost supernatural powers. Such an admission would have made his work worthless. Indeed, what's the point of tracking down, following, catching a creature that can just dissipate into thin air whenever, and transport itself anywhere else?

But, for all of his prejudices, he never attempted to go against proven facts. I remember how he, a green neophyte, convinced me to join the investigation of Matuku Island tragedies.

That case was, of course, under the purview of the Oceania Sector, which didn't want to hear a single word about Wanderers. But the case was unique, with no past precedent (and I sincerely hope that nothing similar ever happens again), so they did not object to me and Toivo joining.

Matuku Island was home to an ancient, decrepit radio telescope. It was impossible to discover who built it and why. The island was considered uninhabited, with only occasional visits by groups of dolphineers and the rare couple looking for pearls in the northern coast's clear bays. As we soon found out, however, a double family of bigheads had settled on the island in recent years. (The current generation has started to forget the bigheads already. A reminder: they're a race of intelligent canids from the planet Saraksh, and for a while they were close with humans. These large-headed talking dogs were happy to accompany us throughout space, and even had an embassy of sorts on our planet. Some thirty years ago they left and haven't had contact with humanity since.)

There was a round volcanic bay in the island's south. It was dirty beyond words, the coast overgrown with some disgusting foam. All that filth was apparently organic, as it attracted countless flocks of seabirds. Other than that, the bays were life-less. Even the algae were slow to grow there.

And murders were taking place on this island. People were killing other people, and it was so horrifying that for months nobody dared to report it to the media.

As it soon transpired, the perpetrator—or, rather, the cause—was a giant Silurian mollusk, a prehistoric cephalopod that had settled at the bottom of the volcanic bay some time ago. It was likely brought there by a storm. The monster's biofield, when it would occasionally surface, had a chilling effect on the psyche of higher-cognition animals. Humans in particular experienced a catastrophic drop in the level of their motivations: people within that field became antisocial, became capable of killing a friend for accidentally dropping a shirt into the water. And kill they did.

Well, then Toivo Glumov convinced himself that the mollusk was, as Bromberg predicted, a Monocosm individual in the process of being created. Admittedly, in the beginning, when there were no facts, his arguments did sound convincing (insofar as logic based on a fantastic premise can be convincing). And it was quite something, seeing him retreat step by step under assault by all the facts that shocked experts on cephalopods and paleontology uncovered every day.

The final straw was when a student of biology dug up a thirteenth-century Japanese manuscript in Tokyo, in which this or a similar monster was described (quoting from my diary here):

In the eastern seas, a purple katatsumuritako may be seen pok-ing out of a round thirty-foot shell, with a multitude of long, thin arms, sharp points, and wattles, its eyes looking rotten, the creature covered with polyps. When it surfaces, it lies flat on the water like an island, spreading a stench and defecating a white mass to attract fish and birds. When they come, it grabs them with its arms and consumes them indiscriminately. On moonlit nights, it drifts on the waves, eyes turned to the sky, and contemplates the dark depths it was ejected from. These contemplations are so bleak that horrified people become like tigers.

I remember how, having read that, Toivo sunk into a thoughtful silence for a few minutes, and then sighed—in relief, it seemed to me—and said, "Yes. This isn't it. And that's a good thing, it's too repugnant." In his mind, the Monocosm had to be quite disgusting, but not to this extent. A Monocosm in the image of a Silurian cephalopod did not fit into his worldview. (Just as it, by the way, didn't fit into any worldview of any experts, with its poisonous biofield, expandable carapace, and an individual age of over four hundred million years.)

As such, the first serious case Toivo Glumov worked on ended in nothing. He would draw quite a few more blanks later, and so in mid-'98 he requested permission to work on materials regarding mass phobias. I granted it.

DOCUMENT 3

COMCON-2, Ural-North
Report 011/99
Date: March 20, '99
Author: Inspector T. Glumov
Subject: 009, "The Visit of the Old Lady"
Contents: Cosmophobia, Penguin syndrome

In my analysis of cases of space-related phobias in the last hundred years, it is my conclusion that the so-called Penguin syndrome may be of interest to us within the scope of subject 009.

SOURCES
Möbius, A. Report at the 14th Conference on Cosmopsychology, Riga, '84.
Möbius, A. "Penguin Syndrome," PCP (Problems of Cosmopsychology), issue 42, '84.
Möbius, A. "Further on the Nature of Penguin Syndrome." PCP, issue 44, '85.

REFERENCE
Asmodeus Matthew Möbius, medical doctor, corresponding member of the European Academy of Medical Sciences, director of the Vienna branch of the World Institute of Cosmic Psychopathology. Born 04/26/36 in Innsbruck. Education: psychopathology faculty, Sorbonne; Second Institute of Space Medicine, Moscow; advanced course in toolless aquanautics, Honolulu. Main research interests: cosmo- and aquaphobia in nonprofessionals. Between '81 and '91, deputy chairman of the Central Medical Committee at Space Command. Currently the renowned founder and chair of the so-called polymorphic cosmopsychopathology school.

On October 7, '84, at a cosmopsychology conference in Riga, Dr. Asmodeus Möbius presented a report on a new type of cosmophobia that he termed Penguin syndrome. The phobia was a harmless mental deviation that manifested as persistent nightmares during sleep. As soon as the sufferer falls asleep, he finds himself floating in empty space, helpless and powerless, lonely and forgotten by everyone, at the mercy of soulless, insurmountable powers. Physically he feels torturous suffocation, feels his body burned by piercing, destructive radiation, his bones thin and melt, the brain start to evaporate, he feels unimaginable, indescribable desperation, and then he wakes up.

Dr. Möbius did not consider the illness dangerous because, first, it was not accompanied by any other mental or physical issues and, second, ambulatory psychotherapy was an effective remedy. Penguin syndrome attracted Dr. Möbius's attention mainly because it was a completely new phenomenon, never described by anyone before. It was surprising that the illness affected people of any gender, age, and profession, and it was no less surprising that no link between the syndrome and the sufferer's gene index could be identified.

Interested in the phenomenon's etiology, Dr. Möbius collected about twelve hundred known cases and conducted a multifactor analysis on eighteen parameters. To his satisfaction, he discovered that 78 percent of cases arose in people who had been on long-range spaceflights on Wraith-17/Penguin ships. "I had expected something along these lines," Dr. Möbius announced. "This is not the first case I can remember in which engineers offered us insufficiently tested technology. And that is why I named my discovered symptom after the ship's model: let that be a lesson."

Based on Dr. Möbius's report, the conference in Riga decided to suspend spaceflights of Wraith-17/Penguin ships until the design deficiencies causing the phobia could be eliminated.

1. I established that the Wraith-17/Penguin model underwent the most thorough examination, and no engineering deficiencies

of note were found, so the direct cause of Penguin syndrome's appearance remained shrouded in mystery. (However, out of an abundance of caution, Space Command retired the Penguins from passenger flights and reassigned them to autopilot routes.) Reported cases of Penguin syndrome decreased dramatically, and, as far as I know, the most recent one was thirteen years ago.

Nonetheless, I wasn't satisfied. I was concerned by the 22 percent whose link to Wraith-17/Penguin ships remained unclear. Out of those 22 percent, according to Dr. Möbius's data, 7 percent had definitely never encountered any Penguins, and the remaining 15 percent weren't sure—they either did not remember or never learned the models of ships they traveled by.

Of course, the statistical significance of the hypothesis that Penguins are related to the phobia is clear. On the other hand, 22 percent is no small number. So I again performed a multifactor analysis of the Möbius data, this time with an additional twenty parameters, which I admittedly picked rather at random, not having even an implausible hypothesis in mind. For example, I included parameters such as launch dates with one-month precision, places of birth with regional precision, hobbies with class precision . . . and so on.

Yet the matter turned out to be simple, and only humanity's perpetual belief in the isotropy of the universe had prevented Dr. Möbius from discovering what I found. And it was as follows: Penguin syndrome affected people on spaceflights toward Saula, Redut, and Cassandra—or, in other words, passing through subspace entry sector 41/02.

The Wraith-17/Penguin ships had nothing to do with it. It's just that the majority of ships back then (early '80s) went straight from the launchpad to the routes Earth–Cassandra–Zephyrus and Earth–Redut–EN 2105. At the time, 80 percent of ships on those routes were Penguins. There's the explanation for Dr. Möbius's 78 percent. As for the other 22 percent of those afflicted, 20 percent of them had flown the same routes with other ships, only leaving 2 percent that had never flown anywhere, but that no longer played any important role.

2. Dr. Möbius's data is doubtlessly incomplete. Using the anamneses he collected, as well as data from Space Command archives, I established that 4,512 people had flown return flights on the relevant routes within the relevant period of time, and 183 of those people (mostly crew members) made multiple such flights. More than two-thirds of the group in question never came to attention of Dr. Möbius.

A conclusion presents itself that they were either immune to Penguin syndrome, or for some reason did not see fit to seek medical attention. Thus it seemed of the utmost importance to establish:

- whether the group of people in question had individuals with immunity to the syndrome,
- if such individuals existed, whether it's possible to ascertain the cause of their immunity, or at least the bio-socio-psychological parameters that differentiate these individuals from those afflicted.

I turned to Dr. Möbius himself with these questions. He replied that he had not considered the problem, but intuitively it seemed that such bio-socio-psychological parameters were highly unlikely to exist. In response to my request, he agreed to task one of his laboratories with studying the issue, warning that the results would arrive no sooner than in two or three months.

In order not to lose time, I consulted the medical archives of Space Command and attempted to analyze the data of all 124 pilots that were regularly flying the relevant routes within the relevant period of time. A simple review showed that, at least for pilots, the probability of contracting Penguin syndrome was about one in three, and did not depend on the number of flights through the "dangerous" sector. Therefore it seems likely that: a) two-thirds of the population are immune to Penguin syndrome, and b) an individual lacking immunity will almost certainly become affected. This is why the question of differences between the immune and nonimmune people is of particular interest.

3. I feel it's necessary to fully quote a note Dr. Möbius included in his paper "Further on the Nature of Penguin Syndrome." Dr. Möbius writes:

> I received a curious message from colleague Krivoklykov (Crimean branch of the Second ISM). After the publication of my Riga report, he wrote that he had been having dreams for several months that are unusually similar to the Penguin syndrome nightmares. He feels himself floating in space, far from stars and planets; he sees his own body without feeling it among many celestial objects, real and imagined. However, unlike the Penguin syndrome sufferers, he does not experience any negative emotions. On the contrary, he feels the situation is interesting and pleasant. He imagines that he's an independent celestial body, moving along a trajectory of his own choosing. The movement is pleasant because he's moving toward some goal that promises great interest. The very sight of star clusters twinkling in the depths of space causes him inexplicable delight, and so on. I imagined that colleague Krivoklykov might be some kind of inverse Penguin syndrome case, which would have been of great interest considering the ideas in this paper. I was, however, disappointed to learn that colleague Krivoklykov had never flown on a Wraith-17/Penguin ship. I remain nonetheless hopeful that inverse Penguin syndrome exists as a psychological phenomenon and I would be thankful to any doctor for kindly bringing new data on this to my attention.

REFERENCE

Ivan Georgievich Krivoklykov, shift doctor/psychiatrist on the Lemboi base (EN 2105). During the time period referenced, made multiple flights on the Earth–Redut–EN 2105 route on spaceships of different types. According to the GWI, he is currently on site at the Lemboi base.

During a personal conversation with Dr. Möbius, I found out that he has identified the "positive" inverse case of Penguin syndrome in two more people in recent years. He refused to reveal their identities, citing medical ethics.

I am not confident to comment on the inverse Penguin syndrome in any detail, but it seems obvious to me that there should be significantly more people with such an inversion than it is currently known.

T. Glumov

(END OF DOCUMENT 3)

+ + +

I included document 3 here not simply because it was one of Toivo Glumov's most promising reports. Reading and rereading it, I felt for the first time that we might be on to something, although I couldn't yet imagine that it would start the sequence of events that ultimately led to my role in the Great Revelation.

On March 21, I read Toivo's report on Penguin syndrome.

On March 25, Sorcerer made a scene at the Oddball Institute (I wouldn't find out about it until a few days later).

And on the 27th, Toivo submitted his report regarding fukamiphobia.

DOCUMENT 4

COMCON-2, Ural-North
Report 013/99
Date: March 26, '99
Author: Inspector T. Glumov
Subject: 009, "The Visit of the Old Lady"
Contents: Fukamiphobia, a history of the Amendment to the Law
   on Mandatory Bioblockade

In my analysis of appearances of mass phobias within the last hundred years, I have concluded that events preceding the World Council's approval on 02/02/85 of the famous Amendment to the Law on Mandatory Bioblockade might be of interest to us within the scope of subject 009.

It should be taken into account that:

1. Bioblockade, also known as the Tokyo procedure, has been in systematic use on Earth and in the Periphery for about 150 years. *Bioblockade* is a colloquial term, preferred by journalists. Medical experts call the procedure *fukamization*, in honor of the sisters Natalya and Hoshiko Fukami, the first to provide a theoretical foundation and apply it in practice. Fukamization aims to increase the human body's natural capacity to adapt to its environment (bioadaptation). In its classic form, fukamization is performed on infants, starting with the final stage of intrauterine development. As far as I could ascertain and understand, the procedure consists of two stages.

First, the introduction of UNBLAF serum (the "bacteria of life" culture) improves the natural resistance to all known infections of a viral, bacterial, or sporal nature, as well as to all organic poisons, by several orders of magnitude. (This part is the bioblockade.)

Second, the acceleration of hypothalamic function via microwaves increases by several times the body's ability to adapt to environmental factors such as harsh radiation, harmful composition of gases in the atmosphere, and high temperature. Additionally, the regenerative abilities of internal organs increase by orders of magnitude, the spectrum perceived by the retina increases, psychotherapy abilities improve, and so on.

The complete instructions for fukamization follow below.

2. Fukamization was universally applied until '85 in accordance with the Law on Mandatory Bioblockade. In '82, a proposed amendment was submitted to the World Council that would make fukamization optional for infants born on Earth. The Amendment would replace fukamization with a so-called maturity vaccine that would be applied at the age of sixteen. In '85, the World Council approved the Amendment to the Law on Mandatory Bioblockade by a slim twelve-vote majority. According to the Amendment, fukamization was no longer mandatory and was entirely at the discretion of parents. Individuals who had not undergone fukamization also had the right to refuse the maturity vaccine, but in that case they would lose the ability to work in any fields of high physical and mental stress. According to the GWI, there are currently about one million non-fukamized teenagers on Earth, and about twenty thousand individuals who refused the maturity vaccine.

INSTRUCTIONS for the multistage prenatal and postnatal fukamization of a newborn:

1. Precisely identify the starting point of childbirth using the even integer method. (Recommended diagnostics: NIMB radioimmunity analysis, FDH-4 and FDH-8 sets.)
2. No less than eighteen hours before the initial contractions of uterine muscles, determine *separately* the weight of the fetus and the amniotic fluid.

NOTE: The Lazarevich offset is *mandatory*. Calculation to be performed *exclusively* based on the Bioadaptation Institute's nomogram that take racial differences into account.

3. Determine the necessary dosage of UNBLAF serum. A complete, stable, and long-lasting immunization against protein agents, as well as protein-like and haptoid structures, is achieved at the dosage of 6.8 gamma-moles per one gram of lymphoid tissue.

   NOTE: a) at volume indexes below 3.5, the dosage is increased by 16 percent, and b) in multiple pregnancies the total dosage is decreased by 8 percent for each additional fetus (twins: 8 percent, triplets: 16 percent, and so on).

4. Six hours before the initial contractions of uterine muscles, use a null-injector to introduce the calculated dose of UNBLAF serum through the front abdominal wall and into the amniotic sac. The injection is to be performed on the side opposite the fetus's back.

5. Fifteen minutes after birth, perform a scintigraphy of the thymus. At thymus indices below 3.8, introduce an additional 2.6 gamma-moles of UNBLAF-11 serum through the umbilical vein.

6. If the body temperature rises, *immediately* place the newborn into a sterile incubator. The first breast-feeding is permissible no sooner than after twelve hours of normal body temperature.

7. Seventy-two hours after birth, perform a microwave acceleration of the adaptogenic zones of the hypothalamus. The topography of the zones is identified via the program BINAR-1. The volumes of the hypothalamic zones should be within the following ranges:

   Zone I: 36–42 neurons

   Zone II: 178–194 neurons

   Zone III: 125–139 neurons

   Zone IV: 460–510 neurons

   Zone V: 460–510 neurons

   NOTE: When measuring, ensure that the birth hematoma has dissipated *entirely*. The acquired data is entered into

BIOFAC-IMPULSE. *It is strictly prohibited to manually correct the IMPULSE data!*

8. Place the newborn into a BIOFAC-IMPULSE operating chamber. When placing the head, make *especially* sure that the stereotactic deviation is no more than 0.014.

9. Microwave acceleration of adaptogenic zones of the hypothalamus is performed at the second level of deep sleep, which corresponds to 1.8–2.1 mV of EEG alpha rhythms.

10. All calculations are *mandatory* to include into the newborn's personal chart.

With regard to the events that led to the adoption of the Amendment to the Law on Mandatory Bioblockade in February'85, I have established the following.

1. In the century and a half of global fukamization, there have been no known cases of the procedure causing any damage. It is thus unsurprising that, until the spring of '81, it was extraordinarily rare for mothers to refuse fukamization. The vast majority of doctors I consulted had never heard of such cases prior to that date. There had been multiple theoretical and propaganda-like cases of opposition to fukamization. Here are some characteristic publications from our century:

- **C. Debuque, *To Build a Human?* (Lyon, '32):** A posthumous publication of the prominent (now forgotten) anti-eugenicist's last book. The second part of the book is entirely devoted to criticism of fukamization as a "shamelessly insidious intrusion into the natural state of the human body." It underscores the irreversibility of fukamization ("nobody has ever managed to decelerate an accelerated hypothalamus"), but the main emphasis is on this typically eugenicist procedure, backed by the power of global law, serving for many years as a bad and enticing example for new experiments in eugenics.

- **K. Pumivur, *Reader: Rights and Duties* (Bangkok, '15):** The author was the vice president of the World Association of

Readers, a proponent and advocate of maximum Reader participation in humanity's affairs. He is against fukamization based on personal statistical data. According to him, fukamization supposedly negatively affects people's Reader potential, and even though the relative proportion of Readers has not decreased in the fukamization era, no new Readers have appeared with powers comparable to Readers of the late twenty-first and early twenty-second century. The author calls for mandatory fukamization to be abolished, at least for the children and grandchildren of Readers. (The book's data is hopelessly out of date—in the '30s, a prominent series of Readers with incredible powers emerged: Alexander Solemba, Peter Dzomny, and others).

- **August Xesis, "The Stumbling Stone" (Athens, '37):** A known theorist and missionary of noophilia, he devoted this pamphlet to scathing criticism of fukamization, but criticism of a more poetic than rational nature. Within the framework of noophilia as some kind of vulgarized Yakowitz theory, the Universe is a container for the Noocosmos, into which the mental and emotional code of an individual flows after death. By all indications, Xesis understands absolutely nothing about fukamization, imagines it to be something like an appendectomy, and passionately calls for the refusal of such a barbaric procedure that damages and perverts the mental and emotional code. (According to the GWI, after the Amendment passed, nobody from the noophilist congregation agreed to the fukamization of their children.)

- **J. Toseville, *Homo impudent* (Birmingham, '51):** This monograph is a rather typical example of an entire library of books and pamphlets advocating the cessation of technological progress. All such books tend to go into apologetics of stagnant civilizations like the Tagorans or the Leonidan biocivilization. They declare that technological progress on Earth has served its purpose. Humanity's expansion into space is portrayed as some social squander that is bound to turn into bitter disappointment. *Homo sapiens* turns into *Homo impudent*, who chases after quantity of rational and emotional information, only to lose out on quality. (Their idea here is that the information concerning the psychocosm is of far greater quality than information concerning outer space, in the broadest possible sense.) Fukamization is a disservice to humanity exactly because it encourages the transformation from *Homo sapiens* into *Homo impudent*, increasing and stimulating expansionist potential. As a first step, it is proposed to at least stop accelerating the hypothalamus.

- **K. Oxoview,** *Vertical Movement* **(Calcutta, '61):** "K. Oxoview" is a pseudonym for a scientist or a group of scientists who formulated and spread the familiar idea of humanity's so-called vertical progress. I haven't been able to discover the identity behind the pseudonym. I have reasons to believe that K. Oxoview is actually COMCON-1 director G. Komov, or one of his associates at the Academy of Social Forecasting. This book is the first monograph of the verticalists. Chapter 6 is devoted to a detailed study of all facets of fukamization—biological, social, and ethical—from the point of view of vertical progress. The main danger of fukamization lies in the possibility of it introducing uncontrolled changes into a genotype. In support of this, they present, for the first time as far as I could discover, data on multiple cases in which a fukamized organism passed on some of its traits. They declare more than a hundred cases in which the immune system of a fetus, still in the mother's body, started producing antibodies typical of the UNBLAF serum, and more than two hundred cases in which newborns had an accelerated hypothalamus at birth. Moreover, they identified more than thirty cases of such hereditary traits in the third generation.

The work emphasizes that even though such phenomena are not directly dangerous to the vast majority of people, they vividly illustrate the fact that fukamization is much less understood than its adepts suggest. I have to note that the material has been meticulously selected and quite impressively presented. For example, a few memorable paragraphs are devoted to the so-called H-allergics who cannot undergo hypothalamic acceleration. H-allergy is an extremely rare condition, easily detectable in a fetus during pregnancy, and therefore posing no danger. Such newborns simply don't undergo phase two of fukamization. But should an H-allergic inherit an accelerated hypothalamus, medicine would be powerless—an incurable person would have been born. K. Oxoview managed to locate one such case, and he spares no effort in describing it. The author presents an even more apocalyptic view of a future in which humanity, due to fukamization's effects, has split into two genotypes. The monograph was published several times and, it seems, played an important role in public discourse on the Amendment. Still, it's interesting to note that the most recent edition of the book (Los Angeles, '99) does not even mention fukamization. It is to be understood that the author is fully satisfied with the Amendment, and doesn't care about the fate of the 99.9 percent of humanity that continues to choose fukamization for their children.

NOTE: In conclusion of this section, I have to emphasize that I selected the materials herein and annotated them based on their nontriviality from my own point of view. I apologize in advance if my insufficient scholarship causes displeasure.

2. The first evident case of fukamization refusal that spurred a subsequent epidemic of such refusals was registered in the maternity home of the village of K'sava (Equatorial Africa). On 04/17/81, all three women that came in within the same day, independently of one another and in different forms, categorically forbade the medical staff to perform fukamization. Woman A (first birth) justified the refusal as the wishes of her husband, who had recently died in an accident. Woman B (first birth) didn't even try to explain her refusal; any attempts at persuasion caused her to become hysterical. "I don't want it," she would repeat. Woman C (third birth, first time protesting) was very rational and calm, and justified her refusal as not wanting to decide her child's fate without the child's knowledge and consent. "That's not my decision to make," she declared.

(I'm including the justifications here because they're completely typical. With minor variations, these account for 95 percent of refusals. Subject literature uses the following classification.
Type-A refusal: a rational but unverifiable justification, 20 percent. Type-B refusal: pure phobia, hysterical and irrational behavior, 65 percent. Type-C refusal, ethical considerations, 10 percent.
Type-R, for rare: very diverse references to religious circumstance,
adherence to exotic philosophies, and so on, about 5 percent.)

On April 18, the same hospital encountered two more refusals, with the first cases also being reported in other maternity
homes in the region. By the end of the month, there were hundreds of cases across the globe, and on May 5 word was received
of the first off-Earth refusal (Mars, Syrtis Major). This epidemic
of refusals continued until '85, with various surges and declines;
by the time of the Amendment's approval there were about fifty
thousand refusers (approx. 0.1 percent of all new mothers).

The epidemic patterns have been studied thoroughly and at
a high confidence level, but no remotely convincing explanation
for the phenomenon was found.

It was for instance noted that the outbreak seemed to have
two distinct geographic origins, one in Equatorial Africa and
another in Northeastern Siberia. That suggest parallels to be
drawn with the likely origin points of early human migrations,
but this analogy doesn't explain anything either.

Another example. Every woman's refusal was always indepen-
dent, yet it seemed that each refusal would cause subsequent ones
in the same maternity home. That gave rise to the term "N-chain
of refusals," with N sometimes being quite large. The maternity
ward of the Howekaii obstetric clinic experienced a refusal chain
starting 09/11/83 and continuing until 09/21, involving every
new arriving mother and resulting in nineteen refusals in a row.

Some hospitals had multiple recurrences of the epidemic. For
example, the Newborn Palace in Bern experienced twelve separate outbreaks.

Despite all of these cases, the vast majority of Earth's maternity homes had never even heard of the refusal epidemic. It was similarly unheard of on most off-Earth settlements. Those that did experience the epidemic (Syrtis Major, Base Saul, Resort) saw it follow the same patterns as on Earth.

3. A large body of literature has been devoted to the causes of fukamiphobia. I familiarized myself with the most respected works, recommended to me by Professor Dheruyod of the Lhasa Psychology Center. My background is insufficient for a comprehensive review of these works, but my impression is that there exists no generally accepted theory on fukamiphobia. Therefore I will limit myself to the following verbatim excerpt from my conversation with Professor Dheruyod.

Q. Is it possible in your opinion for a healthy and happy person to develop the phobia?
A. Strictly speaking, no. A healthy person develops phobias as a result of excessive physical or psychological stress. Such a person could hardly be called happy. On the other hand, especially in our times, a person might not always recognize their own overexertion . . . they could subjectively perceive themselves as happy and satisfied, so from a layman's perspective there is no explanation for them developing a phobia.
Q. And when it comes to fukamiphobia?
A. You know, in some ways pregnancy remains a mystery even today . . . Suffice it to say, we only recently discovered that a pregnant woman's psyche is of binary nature, the result of intricately complex interactions between the mature adult's psyche and the prenatal fetal psyche, of which we know almost nothing. Factoring in the inevitable stress, the inevitable neurotic phenomena . . . taken together this presents a good soil for phobias. But to conclude that this speculation explains anything at all about this amazing story . . . that would be rash. It would be extremely rash and ill advised.

Q. Do the refusers have any differences compared to other mothers? Physiological, psychological . . . has that been studied?

A. Repeatedly, but no conclusions could be drawn. It has always been my belief that fukamiphobia is a universal phobia, just like null-transportation phobia, for instance. It's just that null-T phobia is very widespread; almost everyone, regardless of gender or profession, is afraid of their first null-T jump, but the fear does not persist. Fukamiphobia is, fortunately, an extremely rare occurrence. I say fortunately because we have not found any treatment for fukamiphobia.

Q. Do I understand correctly, Professor, that there is no specific known underlying cause for fukamiphobia?

A. None we have confidence in. There have been many hypotheses, dozens.

Q. Such as?

A. Such as anti-fukamization propaganda from activists. That could affect an impressionable person, during pregnancy particularly. Or, another example, a hypertrophy of maternal instinct, the extreme compulsion to protect her child from any forces, even beneficial ones. You want to argue otherwise? No need, I agree completely: these hypotheses would, at best, explain a small subset of facts. Nobody has offered an explanation for the refusal chains, or the geographic particularities of the outbreaks. And we're all at a complete loss as to why it started specifically in the spring of '81, both on Earth and far away from it.

Q. But you can explain why it ended in '85?

A. Yes, as it happens. Imagine that, the approval of the Amendment seems to have been decisive in ending the epidemic. Questions still remain, of course, but those are insignificant details.

Q. Would you say the epidemic could have been the result of some careless experiments?

A. The theoretical possibility exists. We attempted to verify this hypothesis at one point. There were no experiments being conducted on Earth that could lead to mass phobias.

And keep in mind that fukamiphobia appeared off-planet at the same time.

Q. What kind of experiments could cause phobias?

A. I wasn't specific enough. I could name a number of different techniques that could cause you, a healthy person, to develop some phobia. Note that I am saying *some* phobia. For example, irradiation with a neutrino concentrate with certain parameters would give you a phobia. But which one? The fear of empty space? The fear of heights? The fear of fear? I couldn't say in advance. As for deliberately causing a phobia as specific as fukamiphobia, the fear of fukamization . . . no, that is out of the question. Unless hypnosis were part of it? But that is impossible to implement practically . . . No, that's not a serious possibility.

4. For all of its geographic (and cosmographic) spread, fukamiphobia remained an extremely rare medical phenomenon and would have been unlikely to cause any legal changes. However, the fukamiphobia epidemic rapidly went from a medical issue to a social one.

- August '81. The first registered protests of fathers, of a localized nature at this point (complaints to local and regional medical centers, some petitions to local councils).
- October '81. The first collective petition of 124 fathers and two obstetricians submitted to the World Council's Committee on the Protection of Motherhood and Infancy.
- December '81. At the 17th World Congress of the Obstetrics Association, a large group of doctors and psychologists speak out against mandatory fukamization for the first time.
- January '82. The VEPI group (abbreviated from the names of its founders) unites doctors, psychologists, sociologist, philosophers, and lawyers. The group initiated the Amendment and was instrumental in getting it approved.
- February '82. The first protests outside the World Council building by opponents of fukamization.

- June '82. A formal opposition to the Law on Mandatory Bioblockade emerges within the Committee on the Protection
  of Motherhood and Infancy.

The later timeline is of no particular interest, in my opinion.
The three and a half years it took the World Council to exhaus-
tively study and approve the Amendment is fairly typical. Less
typical is the ratio of general population to professionals among
supporters of the Amendment. Usually, a new law is supported
by tens of millions of people, represented by a professional group
(lawyers, sociologists, experts on the subject matter) of a few
dozen people. In our case, however, the general movement in
support of the Amendment (refuser mothers, their husbands and
relatives, friends, like-minded supporters, philosophical or religious allies) was never a true mass movement. Its size never
exceeded half a million. As for professionals, the VEPI group
alone consisted of 536 specialists when the Amendment was
approved.

5. After the Amendment's approval, refusals did not stop but did
significantly decrease in number. More important, the very nature
of the epidemic changed in '85. In fact the phenomenon could no
longer be considered an epidemic. Any and all patterns (refusal
chains, geographic concentration) disappeared. Refusals became
random, just individual cases with neither type-A nor type-B justifications being prevalent. Refusers would instead invoke the
Amendment explicitly. As a result, doctors no longer consider
fukamization refusals as a manifestation of fukamiphobia. Nota-
bly, many women who were ardently against fukamization and
actively campaigned for the Amendment seem to have lost interest in the issue, and don't even invoke the Amendment when giving birth. Out of the women who refused fukamization between
'81 and '85, only 12 percent refused in a later pregnancy. Three
refusals by the same woman are very rare, with only a handful
of known cases in fifteen years.

6. I consider it necessary to emphasize two points.

a) The near complete disappearance of fukamiphobia after
the Amendment is explainable by well-known psychosocial
factors. A modern person accepts only those restrictions
and obligations that stem from society's moral and ethical
stance. Any other restriction or obligation is perceived with
a (subconscious) dislike and (instinctive) inner protest. It is
natural that, having made fukamization a voluntary choice,
people lose the reason for their dislike of it and start treating
fukamization as any other medical procedure.

Fully accepting and understanding these considerations,
I nonetheless emphasize the possibility of another interpretation within the scope of subject 009. Namely, the entire
described history of fukamiphobia's appearance and disappearance is explainable as a purposeful and calculated interference by some intelligence.

b) The timeframe of the fukamiphobia epidemic matches that
of Penguin syndrome (see my report 011/99).

Sapienti sat.

T. Glumov

(END OF DOCUMENT 4)

✦✦✦

I can now with certainty state that this report by Toivo Glumov
caused the shift in my thinking that finally led me to the Great
Revelation. And, as funny as it seems now, the shift began with
my involuntary irritation at Glumov's crude and unambiguous
hints about the supposed sinister role the "verticalists" played in
the Amendment's history. I struck many parts of that paragraph
in the original document, and I remember planning to chew
Toivo out for his unbridled imagination. Then I got word of

Sorcerer's visit at the Oddball Institute, and a revelation finally dawned on me, all thought of chewing out gone.

I found myself in a deep crisis, because I had no one to talk to. First, I had no specific proposals. Second, I didn't know whom I could still talk to, and who was no longer an option. Much later I asked my team if something had seemed off about my behavior in those horrible (for me) days of April '99. Sandro was up to his eyeballs in "Rip Van Winkle" investigations, too confused himself to have noticed anything. Grisha Serosovin claimed that I had been prone to silence and responded to all of his proposals with a mysterious smile. And Kikin, true to himself, thought it "was obvious" already. Toivo Glumov must have been furious at my behavior then. And he was. But I really had no idea what to do! I sent my employees to the Oddball Institute one after another, waiting for something to happen every time; nothing ever did, so I would send the next one and wait.

At that time, Gorbovsky was dying at home in Krāslava.

At that time, Athos-Sidorov was preparing to go the hospital, and nobody knew if he'd ever leave.

At that time, Daniel Logovenko invited himself over for a cup of tea for the first time in years, and reminisced for a whole evening, chatting about nothing in particular.

At that time, I had not yet decided anything.

And then something went down in Malaya Pesha.

In the early hours of May 6, the emergency group woke me up. Some kind of monsters had appeared, causing total panic in the village of Malaya Pesha (on the Pesha River, falling into the Chosha Bay of the Barents Sea). The emergency group was on its way, conducting an investigation.

According to protocols, I had to send one of my inspectors to the site. I sent Toivo.

Unfortunately, Inspector Glumov's report on the events and his actions in Malaya Pesha has been lost. At least, I was unable to locate it. I would like to show in all possible detail how Toivo conducted the investigation, so I will have to resort to a reconstruction of events, based on my own memory and subsequent conversations with the participants. It will be evident that this reconstruction (and the later ones) contain not only certain facts but also some descriptions, metaphors, epithets, dialogues, and other elements typical of literary fiction. After all, I need the reader to imagine the living Toivo as I remember him. Reports alone won't do. You could choose to view my reconstructions as a particular kind of testimony if you wish.

MALAYA PESHA. MAY 6, '99, EARLY MORNING

From above, the village of Malaya Pesha looked just like it should past three o'clock in the morning. Sleepy. Peaceful. Empty. About a dozen roofs of different colors in a semicircle, a square overgrown with grass, a few scattered gliders, a yellow clubhouse on a cliff above the river. The river appeared motionless, very cold and unwelcoming. Clumps of white fog hovered above the deergrass on the opposite coast.

A man stood on the porch of the clubhouse, his head raised to watch the glider. Toivo thought his face seemed familiar, and that was not surprising—Toivo knew many of the emergency fellows, probably a good half of them.

He set the vehicle down next to the porch and jumped out onto the moist grass. It was a cold morning. The emergency staffer was wearing a huge, cozy overcoat with many special pockets, sockets for balloons, regulators, heaters, and other items the emergency group needed to excel at their work.

"Good morning," Toivo said. "It's Basil, right?"

"Good morning, Glumov," the other responded, offering his hand, "Yes, I'm Basil. What took you so long?"

Toivo explained that the null-T connection to Malaya Pesha had somehow been severed. He got transported to Nizhnyaya Pesha instead, then had to get a glider there and fly for another forty minutes along the river.

"I see." Basil looked back at the clubhouse. "I suspected as much. They smashed the null-T booth up so hard in the panic."

"So nobody has returned yet?"

"Nobody."

"And nothing has happened since?"

44

"Nothing. Our guys finished their survey of the area an hour and a half ago, found nothing significant, and went back to run lab tests. They left me here to keep people away, and I've been repairing the null-T booth."

"Have you repaired it?"

"It's more fixed than broken."

The cottages in Malaya Pesha were old, last-century buildings. Utilitarian architecture, faux natural organics, colors that time had turned into toxic brightness. Each cottage was surrounded by impassable hedges of black currant, lilac, and Arctic strawberries, and beyond the semicircle of houses rose a forest with yellow trunks of giant pines, their crowns a graying green in the fog. Above them, getting higher in the southeast, the sun shone crimson.

"What kind of lab tests?" Toivo asked.

"Well, there's a lot of residue left . . . The vermin apparently crawled out of that cottage and then went everywhere." Basil tried to show with his hands: "In the bushes, on the grass, sometimes on porches, we found dried-up slime, some scales, balls of something . . ."

"What did you see personally?"

"Nothing. When we arrived, it looked as it does now, just the fog was lower over the river."

"So no witnesses?"

"First we thought that everyone had fled. Then it turned out that no, that house over there, closest to the coast, is home to a thriving woman of very advanced age, and fleeing never crossed her mind."

"Why?" Toivo asked.

"Not a clue!" Basil replied, spreading his arms, eyebrows raised. "Can you imagine? Panic all around, everyone's dashing to and fro in terror, door to the null-T booth torn down, and she has not a care in the world. We fly in, full battle gear, swords unsheathed, bayonets fixed—and then she comes out onto the porch and sternly asks us to keep it down, because our hubbub, you see, is keeping her awake!"

"Was there really a panic?" Toivo wondered.

"Hey, hey!" Basil raised his hand. "There were eighteen people here when it all started. Nine people bugged out in gliders. Five fled through the booth. Three ran into the woods, beside themselves—we barely found them. Don't doubt it, there was a panic, there was . . . the panic, the monsters, the residue. We don't know why the old lady didn't get scared. She's strange, this old lady. I heard it myself as she told the commander, 'You're too late, my dears. You cannot help them anymore, they are all dead . . .'"

Toivo asked, "What did she mean by that?"

"I don't know." Basil looked grumpy. "I'm telling you, she's one strange old lady."

Toivo looked toward the toxic-pink cottage housing the strange old lady. Its garden looked much better kept than most. A glider stood next to the cottage.

"I would advise against disturbing her," Basil said. "Let her wake up, and then—"

In that instant, Toivo sensed movement behind him and turned sharply. An ashen face with wide, fearful eyes was staring out of the clubhouse doors. The stranger remained silent for a few seconds, then his blue lips moved and he rasped, "What a silly story, right?"

"Hang on there," Basil spoke kindly, moving toward him with outstretched palms. "I'm very sorry, but you are not allowed here. We're the emergency group."

The stranger nonetheless stepped over the threshold, stopping just outside.

"Well, I'm not really eager to," he coughed, "but the circumstances here . . . Can you tell me if Grigory and Elya are back yet?"

His appearance was rather unusual. He wore a wolfskin fur coat, embroidered fur boots peeking out underneath. The coat was unbuttoned, revealing a many-colored micromesh summer shirt such as was popular in the steppes. The man looked to be in his early forties, a simple kindly face but too white, either from fear or from embarrassment.

"No, no," Basil replied, moving right up to him, "Nobody has returned. We're running an investigation and we're not letting anyone in here."

"Wait, Basil," Toivo said. "Who are Grigory and Elya?" he asked the stranger.

"Oh, I must have ended up in the wrong place again," the stranger sighed with some desperation, and looked behind him at the smooth surface of the null-T booth shining deep in the clubhouse. "Sorry, is this, um, oh my, I forgot again . . . Malaya Pesha? Or not?"

"This is Malaya Pesha," Toivo said.

"Then you should know. Grigory Alexandrovich Yarygin, who lives here every summer as far as I understand." Suddenly he cried out, pointing in excitement: "Look, that cottage there! That's my coat out in the front!"

Things cleared up right away. The stranger was a witness. His name was Anatoly Sergeyevich Krylenko, he was a zootechnician and indeed he worked in the steppes, in the Arzgirsky Agrocomplex specifically. Yesterday, at the yearly exhibition of novelties in Arkhangel'sk, by pure chance he ran into his old school friend Grigory Yarygin. They hadn't seen each other in about a decade. Of course, Yarygin took him here to this . . . forgot again . . . right, Malaya Pesha. The three of them—he, Yarygin, and his wife Elya—spent an excellent evening boating and walking in the woods, returned home, to that cottage over there, at about ten in the evening, had dinner, and settled out front to have tea. It was light outside, children's voices were coming from the river, it was pleasantly warm, the smell of Arctic strawberries pleasant in the air . . . and then Anatoly Sergeyevich Krylenko saw eyes.

At this most relevant point of his story, Anatoly Sergeyevich became incoherent, to put it mildly. It was as if he was trying to recount some convoluted, terrifying nightmare.

The eyes were staring from the garden. They were coming closer, but remained in the garden. Two huge, nauseating eyes. Something was dripping over them. On the left, there was a third . . . or three more? Something was falling, stumbling, lumbering over the rails and flowing toward the steps. It was impossible to move. Grigory gone somewhere—no sight of Grigory. Elya was somewhere here, but no sight of her either, just her hysterical shrieks . . . or laughter? The door burst open. The room was filled to the waist with moving, viscid flesh, but the eyes of the flesh remained out there, behind the bushes . . .

Then Anatoly Sergeyevich realized that something worse was about to begin. He tore his feet out of sandals that had gotten stuck to the floor, jumped over the table, stumbled into the woods, ran around the house . . . No, he didn't . . . Strange, he went into the woods but somehow ended up in the square . . . He ran where his feet took him and finally saw the clubhouse, a purple null-T flash visible through its open doors, and he knew he was saved. He barged into the booth and pressed buttons at random until the device activated.

Thus concluded the tragedy, and then the comedy began. The null-transporter ejected Anatoly Sergeyevich in the village of Roosevelt on Peter I Island. That's in the Bellingshausen Sea, minus fifty-six degrees, wind gusts of thirty-five knots, the village empty as usual in winter.

The machinery at the polar clubhouse is working just fine: it is warm and homely, the bar an inviting rainbow of bottles with liquids that can brighten up Arctic nights. Anatoly Sergeyevich, in his motley shirt and shorts, still dripping with sweat after the tea and the later horror, gets a much-needed break and begins to regain composure. When he comes to his senses, his first feeling is unsurprisingly that of unbearable shame. He understands that he had fled in panic like a complete coward, the kind of which he had only read about in historical novels. He remembers that he abandoned Elya and at least one more woman he caught a glimpse of in the cottage next door. He remembers children's voices coming from the river and realizes he abandoned those children as well. He is consumed by a desperate compulsion to act, but the compulsion does not arise immediately, and when it finally does, it is matched by intolerable horror at the very idea of going back there, into the view of those nightmarish dripping eyes, the revolting viscid flesh.

A loud gaggle of glacial explorers who barged into the clubhouse from the freezing cold found Anatoly Sergeyevich wringing his hands in misery as he failed to make up his mind. The explorers listened to him with empathy and enthusiastically agreed to accompany him back to the terrifying cottage veranda. It immediately transpired, however, that Anatoly Sergeyevich not only didn't know the village's null-T index but had forgotten its very name. He could only say it was near the Barents Sea, on the coast of a small river with an Arctic pine forest. The glaciologists hurriedly dressed Anatoly Sergeyevich into something more weather appropriate and dragged him through a raging blizzard to the local headquarters, accompanied by giant beastly dogs and cutting straight through monstrous snowdrifts. There in the headquarters, in front of a GWI terminal, one of the polar explorers had the sensible thought that this was no laughing matter. The monsters had clearly broken out of some menagerie or—terrifying to even consider—some biomechanism construction laboratory. Either way, this didn't call for a spontaneous response by a bunch of friends; the emergency group had to be notified.

And so they notified Central Emergency. Central thanked them and took the report under advisement. Half an hour later, an emergency dispatcher called the polar headquarters, said the report had been confirmed, and asked to talk to Anatoly Sergeyevich. He explained in general terms what had happened and how he ended up next to Antarctica. The dispatcher calmed him down in the sense that there were no victims, the Yarygins were alive and well, and Malaya Pesha should be safe to return to by morning, but for now Anatoly Sergeyevich's best course of action would be to take some sedatives and lie down.

Anatoly Sergeyevich did take sedatives and did nap right there on the couch—but had slept for less than an hour when he again saw the eyes dripping over the railings, heard Elya's mad laughter, and woke up in unbearable shame.

"No," Anatoly Sergeyevich said, "they did not try to keep me there. They must have understood my state of mind. I could have never imagined something like that happening to me! I am, of course, no pathfinder or progressor, but I have had my difficult moments in life and I always carried myself honorably. I do not understand what happened to me. I'm trying to explain it to myself, but I cannot. It's like some delusion." His eyes started darting. "Even now I'm talking to you, but my insides are all cold. Maybe we all got poisoned here?"

"Could it possibly have been a hallucination?" Toivo asked.

Anatoly Sergeyevich gave a chilly shrug and glanced toward the Yarygin cottage. "I'm no– . . . not sure," he managed. "No, I really can't say."

"All right, let's go take a look," Toivo offered.

"Should I come with you?" Basil asked.

"No need," Toivo said. "I will take a while walking around. You hold down the fort."

"Should I take prisoners?" Basil asked, businesslike.

"Definitely," Toivo said. "I need prisoners. Anyone who has seen anything at all."

So he and Anatoly Sergeyevich set out, walking across the square. Anatoly Sergeyevich looked serious and decisive, but the closer he came to the cottage, the tenser he became, clenching his jaw and biting his lower lip as if not to cry out in pain. Toivo felt it necessary to give him a break. Some fifty steps from the hedges, he stopped, pretending to take another look at the surroundings, and began to ask questions. Was there anyone in that cottage on the right? Oh, it was dark . . . On the left, then? A woman . . . Yes, I remember, you mentioned. Just the woman and nobody else? Were there any gliders here?

Toivo kept asking and Anatoly Sergeyevich kept answering; Toivo nodded seriously and made every effort to show how helpful the answers were. Anatoly Sergeyevich gradually cheered up, relaxed, and they stepped onto the veranda almost like two colleagues.

The veranda was in disarray. The table was askew, one of the chairs was flipped over, and the sugar bowl had rolled into a corner, strewing sugar in its path. Toivo touched the teapot—it was still warm. He glanced at Anatoly Sergeyevich. Blood had drained from his face again, and he was clenching his jaws. He was looking at a lonely pair of sandals under the chair farthest away. His own sandals, evidently. They were fastened, and it wasn't clear how Anatoly Sergeyevich could have gotten his feet out of them. Still, Toivo couldn't see any traces on, under, or near them.

"Doesn't look like household robots are popular here," said Toivo seriously, to bring Anatoly Sergeyevich out of the nightmare world into that of mundanity.

"Yes," he muttered. "I mean, where are they popular? See my sandals . . ."

"I see, yes," Toivo responded indifferently. "Were the windows all open like this?"

"I don't remember. That one was at least, I jumped out there."

"Understood," Toivo said, and looked out into the garden.

Yes, there were traces, there were many traces. Torn and flattened bushes, ruined flower beds, and grass under the railings that looked as if horses had lain on it. If any animals had been here, they had to have been clumsy, bulky animals, and they had not been sneaking up to the houses. They had gone in a straight line, from the square, across through the hedges and straight into rooms through open windows.

Toivo crossed the veranda and pushed the cottage door open. There was no disorder there. Or no disorder that giant clumsy bodies should have caused.

A couch. Three chairs. No table in sight—presumably a built-in. Just one control panel, in the armrest of the owner's chair.

Polycrystal service systems in the other chairs and in the couch. A Levitan painting on the front wall, an ancient chromophotonic copy with a touching little triangle in the bottom left corner to spare some art connoisseur from taking it for an original. On the left wall, a quill drawing of an angry female face in a homemade wooden frame. A nonetheless pretty face . . .

In a more thorough examination, Toivo discovered boot prints on the floor. One of the emergency crew had probably carefully stepped through here and into the bedroom. No prints in the opposite direction, meaning he climbed out the bedroom window. The living room floor was covered in a fairly thick layer of very fine brown dust. And not only the floor. Chair seats. Windowsills. The couch. No dust on the walls.

Toivo returned to the veranda to find Anatoly Sergeyevich sitting on the porch steps. He had thrown off his wolfskin coat but forgot to take the fur boots off, making him look rather ridiculous. His sandals were still under the chair, untouched. No traces of anything in the vicinity, but the sandals and the floor next to them were covered in that same brown dust.

"How are you doing here?" Toivo asked from the doorway.

Anatoly Sergeyevich sharply turned, startled. "Well . . . coming to, slowly."

"That's great. Take your coat and head home. Or would you prefer to wait for the Yarygins?"

"I'm not sure," said Anatoly Sergeyevich indecisively.

"As you wish," Toivo said. "There is and will be no danger here in any case."

"Have you figured something out?" Anatoly Sergeyevich rose to his feet.

"A bit. There were monsters here, indeed, but they really were harmless. They can frighten, but no more than that."

"Are you saying that it was artificial?"

"Looks like it."

"But why? Who?"

"We'll find out," said Toivo.

"While you're finding out, they will give someone else . . . a scare."

Anatoly Sergeyevich took his coat from the railing and stood, looking at his fur boots. It looked like he was about to sit down and angrily tear them off, but he probably couldn't even see them.

"You say they can frighten . . ." He didn't lift his eyes as he spoke through gritted teeth. "If only that was it! They can, you know, destroy!"

He shot a quick glance at Toivo and then, without turning back, went down the steps and on, over flattened grass, through the ruined hedges, across through the square, hunched over, looking ridiculous in polar fur boots and the merry bright shirt of a farmer; he walked away, faster with every step, toward the yellow clubhouse. Halfway there, he sharply turned left, jumped into a glider in front of the next cottage, and took straight off into the pale blue sky.

It was past four in the morning.

✦✦✦

The above constitutes my first attempt at a reconstruction. I did my best. It was harder because I never went to Malaya Pesha, not back in the day, but I had access to a sufficient number of recordings made by Toivo Glumov, the emergency group, and Fleming's crew. So I'm confident when it comes to the topography, at least. I can also vouch for the accuracy of the dialogues.

Aside from all that, I also wanted to show what a typical beginning of a typical investigation looked like back then. Some event. Emergency group. Arrival of an inspector from the UE Department. The first impression (that would usually prove to be correct) that it's someone's negligence or stupid joke. And growing disappointment—this isn't it, again, yet another blank, would rather forget it all and go home for a nap . . . but there's none of that in my reconstruction. You can fill those gaps with your imagination.

Now, a few words about Fleming.

The name makes a few appearances in my memoir, but I want to say right away that the man had nothing to do with the Great Revelation. At that time, the name Alexander Jonathan Fleming was the talk of the town at COMCON-2. He was the leading expert on the construction of artificial organisms. At his main institute in Sydney, and its many branches, he would combine indescribable dedication with audacity to cook up a variety of outrageous creatures that Mother Nature lacked the imagination to create. In their zeal, his employees would constantly break the World Council's laws and limitations on experimentation. For all our involuntary admiration of Fleming's genius on a personal level, we couldn't stand him for his unapologetic, shameless assertiveness that, amazingly, coexisted with evasiveness. Today, every schoolboy knows what a Fleming biocomplex is, or, for instance, a Fleming living fountain. Back in the day, he had more notoriety than fame among the general public.

For my story, it is relevant that one of remote branches of Fleming's Sydney institute was located at the mouth of the Pesha River, in the Nizhnyaya Pesha scientific village, a mere twenty-five miles from Malaya Pesha. When my dear Toivo found that out, he of course couldn't prevent himself from getting suspicious and thinking, So that's whose handiwork it was!

Oh, by the way, the craycrabs mentioned below are one of Fleming's most useful creations, which first appeared back when he was a young worker at a fishery on Lake Onega. The craycrabs turned out to taste fantastic, but for some reason never thrived in the North, except in the small streams flowing into the Pesha River.

MALAYA PESHA, MAY 6, '99, SIX IN THE MORNING

On May 5, the summer cottage village of Malaya Pesha (thirteen cottages, total population eighteen) was consumed by panic. The panic was caused by the appearance of an unknown number of quasibiological creatures of extremely repulsive and even frightening appearance. The creatures moved into the village out of cottage #7 following nine clearly identifiable paths. The paths can be tracked by flattened grass, damaged bushes, and dried slime on the shrubbery, on cladding, on the outer walls of buildings, and on windowsills. All nine paths terminate in living spaces—specifically, in cottages #1, #4, #10 (on verandas); #2, #3, #9, #12 (in living rooms); #6 and #13 (in bedrooms). Cottages #4 and #9 appear uninhabited.

As for cottage #7, where the invasion came from, someone clearly lived there, and the question was who—a stupid joker or an irresponsible bungler? Did that person release embryophores intentionally, or fail to notice their escape? And in the latter case, was it criminal negligence or ignorance?

Two issues caused confusion here. Toivo did not find any traces of embryophore shells. That's the first problem. And second, he initially failed to locate any information about the inhabitant or inhabitants of cottage #7.

Fortunately, our ecumene is in general quite just. Loud, angry voices suddenly rose from the square, and a minute later it was clear that the sought-after inhabitant had turned up front and center, personally, and even brought a guest.

The person turned out to be a stocky man with a cast-iron appearance, wearing travel overalls and carrying a canvas bag from which strange hissing and screeching emerged. The man's guest made Toivo think of the character of good old Duremar straight out of Tortila's pond: tall, long-haired, thin, long-nosed, in unidentifiable robes covered with drying seaweed. It transpired that the cast-iron inhabitant was one Ernst Jürgen, working as an orthomaster operator on Titan, vacationing here on Earth. He vacations on Earth every year for two months, once in summer and once in winter, and every summer it's here, on the Pesha River, in this very cottage. What monsters? Whom are you talking about, young man? What monsters can there be in Malaya Pesha, what are you thinking? You call yourself the emergency crew, have you nothing better to do?

Duremar, on the contrary, was very much an Earth creature. An almost local creature at that. Last name Tolstov, name Leo Nikolayevich. That wasn't the most wondrous thing about him. He, it turns out, resides and works just twenty-five miles from here, in Nizhnyaya Pesha, where for a few years now a small little branch of a certain Fleming's company has quietly operated.

It also transpired that this Ernst Jürgen and his old friend Leo Tolstov were real gourmets. They meet yearly here, in Malaya Pesha, because just three miles upstream a small tributary feeds into the Pesha and is home to something called craycrabs. And that is why he, Ernst Jürgen, spends his vacation in Malaya Pesha, and that is why he and his friend Leo Tolstov departed yesterday evening on a boat to fish for craycrabs, and that is why he and Leo would very much appreciate if the emergency group could leave them alone right about now, because with craycrabs (here Ernst Jürgen shook the heavy bag that produced weird noises) there is only one freshness—the first. The funny loud man couldn't imagine that on Earth—not on his Titan, not somewhere on Pandora, not on Yaila—no, on Earth!—Malaya Pesha of all places could see events that cause fear and panic.

A very curious type, these professional space explorers. He sees the village is empty, he sees an emergency group member, he sees a COMCON-2 representative, and he doesn't deny their authority, but he's ready to look for any explanation that doesn't imply that Earth, his native hearth, could have trouble. When he was finally convinced that there had indeed been a UE, he sulked—got sad like a child, pouted, and went away, dragging his precious craycrab bag behind him, and set himself down next to it on his porch, not wanting to face anyone, not wanting to see anyone or hear anything, occasionally shrugging and growling, "Some vacation I took . . . come here once a year, and still . . . just imagine this here!"

Toivo was more interested in the reaction of his friend, Leo Nikolayevich Tolstov, Fleming's employee, an expert on constructing artificial organisms and launching them into existence. And the specialist's reaction was this: First, total confusion, batting eyes with the uncertain smile of a person suspecting a prank, and a silly one at that. Then, a pensive frown, an empty stare seemingly turned inward, and brooding lower jaw movements. And finally, a flash of professional indignation. Do you even understand what you're saying? Do you have any conception of the subject? Have you even seen an artificial creature? Oh, just in the chronicles? So get this, there are not and cannot be any artificial creatures that would be capable of crawling through windows and into bedrooms. First of all, they are slow, clumsy, and when they do move it's away from people, not toward, because they're repelled by natural biofields, even a cat's. Then, what nonsense is "the size of a cow"? Go and at least roughly estimate the energy an embryophore would need to reach such mass, even if it took an hour. There would be nothing left of this place, not a single cow either—it would simply be an explosion!

Would he consider the possibility that embryophores of a type unknown to him were active here?

Not in the slightest. Such embryophores do not exist.

What happened here then, according to him?

Leo Tolstov didn't know what had happened. He needed to look around to reach any conclusions.

Toivo left him to have a look, and headed to the clubhouse with Basil to have a bite to eat. They had a cold meat sandwich each, and Toivo got to work on brewing coffee. And then . . .

"*Mmmm!*" Basil suddenly pronounced, his mouth full.

He swallowed mightily and, looking past Toivo, barked, "Hold it there! Where are you going, son?"

Toivo turned. There was a boy of about twelve, tanned and lop-eared, wearing shorts and a shirt with no buttons. Basil's mighty shout stopped him just at the clubhouse door.

"Home," he said, as if in challenge.

"Well, would you come here, please!" Basil asked.

The boy approached and stood, arms behind his back.

"Do you live here?" Basil attempted to gain trust.

"We did," replied the boy. "In number six. Now we won't."

"Who is *we?*" asked Toivo.

"Me, mother, and father. Or, we were here in our summer house. We live in Petrozavodsk."

"And where are your parents now?"

"At home. Sleeping."

"Sleeping," Toivo repeated. "What's your name?"

"Kir."

"Do your parents know you're here?"

Kir hesitated, shuffled from one foot to another. "I just came in for a moment. I need to get my galley—I spent a month building it."

"Galley," Toivo repeated, watching the boy.

The boy's face expressed only patient boredom. He clearly had just one concern: to get his galley as soon as possible and get home before his parents woke up.

"When did you leave here?"

"Last night. Everyone was leaving. We did as well. But we forgot the galley."

"Why did you leave, then?"

"There was a panic. Don't you know? That was something! Mom got frightened, and father said, all right, let's all go home.

We got into a glider and flew away. So I'll get going, then? Or is it forbidden?"

"Wait a minute. Why do you think there was a panic?"

"Because those animals came. Out of the woods, or the river. Everyone got so scared for some reason, started running around . . . I was asleep, Mom woke me up."

"Didn't you get frightened?"

He shrugged. "Well, I did at first. I was sleepy, everyone's shouting, screaming, running, can't understand anything . . ."

"And then?"

"I told you, we got into a glider and flew off."

"The animals, did you see them?"

He suddenly laughed. "Sure I did. One climbed right in through the window. It had horns, but they were not hard, like a snail's. Very funny."

"So you didn't get frightened?"

"No, I'm telling you, I was scared. Why would I lie to you? Mom was all pale when she ran in, I thought something bad had happened, to Dad maybe . . ."

"Right, right. But were you not frightened by the animals?"

Kir said, annoyed, "Why would you be afraid of them? They are kind, funny . . . they're soft, silky, like a mongoose but without fur. So what if they're big? Tigers are big, should I be afraid of them? Elephants are big, whales are. Dolphins can be big, and these animals were sure no bigger than dolphins, and just as kind."

Toivo looked at Basil. Basil, his mouth open, was holding a half-eaten sandwich and listening to this strange boy.

"And they smell nice!" Kir sounded passionate. "They smell like berries! I think they eat berries. We should tame them. Why run from them?" He sighed. "They're gone now, I suppose. Go find them out there in the taiga . . . of course! Everyone was shouting at them, stomping their feet, waving their arms! Of course they got scared! Go and try to lure them back now . . ."

He lowered his head in sorrowful thought. Toivo said, "I understand. But your parents don't agree with you, right?"

Kir waved the suggestion away. "Yes, well . . . Father isn't that bad, but Mom is so firm—never again, won't step foot here, no matter what! And now we're flying to Resort. And these animals don't live there . . . or do they? Do you know what they're called?"

"I don't know, Kir," Toivo said.

"But there aren't any of them here?"

"No, none."

"Just as I thought," said Kir. He sighed again and asked, "May I get my galley?"

Basil finally came to his senses. He rose noisily and said, "Let's go, I'll go with you. Right?" He looked at Toivo.

"Of course."

"Why walk me there?" Kir got frustrated, but Basil already had an arm on his shoulder.

"Let's go, let's go," he said. "I've always wanted to see a real galley."

"It's not, it's a model."

"Even better. I've always wanted to see a model of a real galley."

They left. Toivo had a cup of coffee and also left the clubhouse.

The sun was noticeably warm; the sky cloudless. Blue dragonflies flickered above the magnificent grass of the square. And through their metallic flickering, like a striking daytime ghost, a majestic old woman floated toward the clubhouse, her narrow brown face completely standoffish.

Her brown, birdlike hand holding (with a devilish elegance) the rim of a subdued snow-white dress, she, as if not touching the grass, floated up to Toivo and stopped, towering above him. Toivo bowed respectfully, and she nodded in response, although benevolently.

"You may call me Albina," she allowed in a pleasant baritone.

Toivo hurried to introduce himself.

She furrowed her brown brow below a rich crown of white hair. "COMCON? Well then, let it be COMCON. Would you be so kind, Toivo, as to tell me how you at COMCON explain all of this?"

"What exactly do you mean?" Toivo asked.

The question irritated her somewhat. "I mean, my dear, this," she said. "How could it come to pass that in our age, at the end of this century, here on Earth, living creatures called upon humanity for help and compassion, but not only did they receive no help or compassion, they were made victims of persecution, threats, and even active physical impact of the most barbaric nature? I do not wish to name anyone, but they hit them with rakes, they shouted madly, they even tried to run them over with gliders. I would have never believed it, had I not seen with my own eyes. Are you familiar with the concept of savagery? That was savagery! I am ashamed."

She fell silent, not taking her piercing, coal-black, and very young eyes off Toivo.

She was waiting for a response, and Toivo muttered, "Would you allow me to bring out a chair for you?"

"I will not," she said. "I am not going to have a sit-down with you here. I would wish to hear your opinion on what happened to the people in this village. Your professional opinion. Who are you? A sociologist? Teacher? Psychologist? Well then, do me the courtesy of explaining! I am not talking about punishments here. But we have to understand how this could happen, how people who yesterday were still civilized, well-raised, I would even say excellent people, how they could today have lost their humanity. Do you know what separates humans from all other beings?"

"Uh, intelligence?" Toivo guessed at random.

"No, dear. Compassion! *Com-pas-sion!*"

"But of course," Toivo said. "How does it follow, though, that the creatures here were in need of compassion?"

She shot him a disgusted look. "Did you see them personally?" she asked.

"No."

"Then how can you judge?"

"I am not judging," Toivo said. "I am trying to find out what they were after."

"I think I was quite clear in telling you that these living creatures, these poor things, were looking for our help! They were on the verge of death! They had to be dying! They did die, don't you know that? Every single one of them! They were dying in front of my eyes, turning to nothing, to dust, and I couldn't help—I am a ballerina, not a biologist, not a doctor. I called out, but could anyone have heard me in this debauchery, in this bacchanalia of savagery and cruelty? And then, when help finally arrived, it was too late—none had survived. None! And those savages . . . I don't know how to explain their behavior. Maybe this was mass psychosis. A poisoning? I've always been against eating mushrooms. I presume, when they came to, they all fled out of shame! Have you found them?"

"Yes," Toivo said.

"Have you spoken to them?"

"Yes. To some. Not all."

"Then do tell me, what happened to them? What are your conclusions, at least preliminarily?"

"You see . . . madam . . ."

"You may call me Albina."

"Thank you. You see, the thing here . . . the thing is, as far as we can conclude, the majority of your neighbors perceived this invas– . . . this event somewhat differently than you did."

"Of course," Albina said arrogantly. "I saw it myself!"

"No, no. What I want to say is, they got frightened. They were mortally terrified. They were beyond themselves with horror. They are afraid to even return here. Some want to flee Earth after what they saw. And as far as I understand, you are the only person who heard cries for help."

She listened majestically but attentively. "Well then," she offered, "it seems they are so ashamed that they have to excuse it with fear. Do not believe them, my dear, do not! This was very primitive, the most shameful kind of xenophobia. Just like racial prejudice. I remember, as a child I was hysterically afraid of spiders and snakes. This is the same."

"That could well be true. But I'd like to clarify one point. They were asking for help, the creatures. They required compassion. But how did that manifest? I understand that they did not talk, or moan even?"

"My dear! They were sick, they were dying! So what if they were dying silently? A beached dolphin also makes no sound, none that we can hear at least. But it is plain to us that it requires help, and we hurry to provide it. There goes a boy: you don't hear what he is saying from here, but you can clearly see that he's alert, joyful, and happy."

Kir was approaching from cottage number six, and he was indeed clearly alert, joyful, and happy. Basil walked alongside him, respectfully carrying a large black model of an antique galley, and seemed to be asking appropriate questions, which Kir answered, indicating dimensions and shapes with his hands, explaining complex interactions. Basil really did look like an enthusiast of antique galley models.

"Pardon me," said Albina, squinting, "but that is Kir!"

"Yes," Toivo said, "he returned for his model."

"Kir is a good boy," Albina declared, "but his father's behavior was revolting. Good morning to you, Kir!"

The excited Kir only now noticed her, stopped, and shyly wished Albina good morning. The high spirits were gone from his face, and Basil's as well.

"How is your mother feeling?" Albina inquired.

"Thanks. She's asleep."

"And your dad? Where is your father, Kir? Is he somewhere here?"

Kir silently shook his head and frowned.

"You stayed here the whole time?" Albina sounded delighted, and looked at Toivo victoriously.

"He returned for his model," he reminded her.

"That does not matter. You were not afraid of returning here, were you, Kir?"

"Why fear them, Grandma Albina?" Kir mumbled resentfully, trying to move around her sideways.

"I don't know, I don't know." Albina was cross. "Your father, for example . . ."

"Dad wasn't afraid at all. Or he was, but only for Mom and me. In all that confusion, he didn't understand how kind they were."

"Miserable, not kind," Albina corrected him.

"Miserable how, Grandma Albina?" Kir protested, spreading his hands like an untrained tragedian. "They were fun, they wanted to play! They were so cuddly!"

Grandma Albina smiled condescendingly.

✦✦✦

I cannot resist noting right here one thing that characterizes Toivo Glumov so well as an agent. A green intern in his place, after talking to Duremar Tolstov, would have decided that he was lying and that everything was perfectly clear. Fleming had created a new type of embryophore, his monsters had broken loose, so it's time to take a nap and afterward report up the chain of command.

And an experienced employee—for example, Sandro Mtbevari—would not have sat down to drink coffee with Basil. A new type of embryophore is no joke. He would have sent twenty-five inquiries to everyone imaginable, and rushed directly off to Nizhnyaya Pesha to grab Fleming's bandits and bunglers by the scruff before they could prepare to look all offended and innocent. But Toivo Glumov didn't move. Why? He had smelled sulfur. Not even a smell—less, he caught a whiff. An unknown embryophore? Yes, of course, that is serious. But that does not smell like sulfur. Hysterical panic? That's closer. Much. But most important, the strange old lady from cottage number one. There! Panic, hysterics, mass flight, emergency crews, and she says to keep it down and let her sleep. That had no traditional explanation. Toivo didn't try to find any. He just stayed there, waiting for her to wake up and to ask her some questions. He stayed and was rewarded. "Had I not thought to have breakfast with Basil," he would later say, "if I had gone to report to you right after talking to this Tolstov, I would have remained under the impression that nothing mysterious had happened in Malaya Pesha, aside from the mad panic caused by artificial animals. And then the boy Kir and Grandma Albina showed up, severely undermining that self-consistent but primitive theory."

"Thought to have breakfast"—that's how he phrased it. Probably to avoid putting into words the unclear feelings of unease that had caused him to stay.

MALAYA PESHA, SAME DAY, EIGHT IN THE MORNING

His galley in tow, Kir somehow squeezed into the null-T booth and was off to Petrozavodsk. Basil took off his monstrous garb, fell onto the grass in the shade, and seemed to sleep. Grandma Albina floated back to cottage number one.

Toivo didn't go into the clubhouse. He just sat down on the grass, legs crossed, and waited.

Nothing of note was happening in Malaya Pesha. Cast-iron Jürgen gave an occasional roar from the depths of his cottage number seven, something about the weather, and the river, and the vacation. Albina, still all in white, came out on her veranda and sat under its roof. The air carried her soft singsong voice—she was on a videophone call. Duremar Tolstov passed in and out of view. He scurried between cottages, occasionally squatting, looking at the ground, digging in the bushes, and occasionally even moved on all fours.

At half past seven, Toivo rose, went into the clubhouse, and videocalled his mother. The usual check-in call. He was worried that the day might be too busy to find another time for a call. They talked about this and that . . . Toivo said that he had met an elderly ballerina by the name of Albina. Couldn't that be Albina the Great, whom he never stopped hearing about as a child? They discussed the question and concluded that it was possible, but there was another great ballerina Albina, fifty years older than Albina the Great. They said good-bye for the day.

A mighty roar came from the outside. "What about the crabs? The crabs, Leo!"

Leo Tolstov was hurriedly approaching the clubhouse, waving his left hand in irritation, his right pressing some big bag to his chest. At the entrance, he paused and shrieked in a whiny

falsetto toward cottage number seven, "I'll be back soon!" Then
he noticed Toivo watching him and explained, as if apologizing,
"One very strange story, this. Have to get it sorted out."

He disappeared into the null-T booth, and events continued
not to occur for a while longer. Toivo decided to wait until eight.

Five minutes to eight, a glider dived out from behind the
woods, flew a few circles above Malaya Pesha, descending
slowly, and made a soft landing in front of cottage number ten,
the same one where, by all appearances, a painter's family lived.
A tall young man jumped out of the glider, lightly ran up the
veranda steps, and shouted, turning back, "It's all right! Nothing
and nobody here!" While Toivo walked toward them across the
square, a young, short-haired woman in an above-the-knee purple
cloak stepped out of the glider. She didn't go toward the porch;
she stood by the glider, holding on to its door.

The painter of the family turned out to be this very woman,
by the name Zosya Lyadova, and it was her self-portrait that
Toivo had seen in the Yarygins' cottage. She was twenty-five or
twenty-six, a student of the Academy, the Komovsky-Korsakov
studio, and had not yet created anything of note. She was beautiful, much more so than her self-portrait. She reminded Toivo of
his Asya somewhat, but he had never seen his Asya so frightened.

The man's name was Oleg Olegovich Pankratov; he was a lecturer in the Syktyvkar region, and for almost thirty years before
that he had been an astroarchaelogist who had worked in Fokin's
group, participated in the expedition to Kala-i Mug (also known
as "the Morohashi paradox planet"), and seen everything under
the blue sky, as well as the green, gray, and many more other
skies. A very calm, even placid man, resilient, reliable, hands the
size of spades, not even a bulldozer could move him. Yet his face
was light, with flushed cheeks, blue eyes, a bulbous nose, and a
huge, fair beard, like Ilya Muromets or other knights of legend.

It was entirely unsurprising that the husband and wife did not
act at all alike during the night's events. Oleg Olegovich, seeing
living sacs stumble in through bedroom windows, was surprised,

of course, but did not feel any fear. Maybe because he thought of the Nizhnyaya Pesha branch right away, having visited it a few times, and the appearance of the monsters did not signal danger to him. Disgust was his main feeling. Disgust and revulsion, yes, but not fear. He held the sacs off with his hands, pushing them back into the garden, and it was vile, sticky, slimy, the sacs felt repulsively soft yet tight, they were like the innards of some giant animal. He dashed across the bedroom, looking for something to clean his hands with, but then Zosya screamed and there was no time for disgust.

Yes, all of us were not on our best behavior, but you can't let yourself go like some did. Some are still not in their right mind. Frolov had to be hospitalized right there in Sula—they had to drag him out of the glider, he was so beyond himself. The Grigoryans, kids and all, wasted no time in Sula: all four of them ran to the null-T cabin and jumped straight to Mirzachirla. Grigoryan shouted by way of a good-bye, "Anywhere that's far and forever away!"

Zosya, on the other hand, understood the Grigoryans quite well. She had never experienced such horror. And it had nothing to do with whether the animals were dangerous or not. "If we were all driven by horror . . . Don't, Oleg, I'm speaking about us, normal unprepared people, not firewalkers like you . . . If we were all driven by horror, it wasn't the fear of being eaten, suffocated, digested, and all that. No, it was an entirely different feeling!" Zosya struggled with choosing any words to describe that feeling. Her most understandable phrasing was that it wasn't a fearful horror, it was a sense of complete incompatibility, the impossibility of being in the same volume of space as those creatures. But there was something more interesting in her retelling.

It turns out that the monsters were also beautiful! They were so scary and disgusting that they seemed to be somehow perfect. Perfect hideousness. The aesthetic juncture of ideal repulsiveness and ideal beauty. Someone once said that perfect hideousness should aesthetically feel the same as perfect beauty. She had thought it a paradox until last night. It was no paradox! Or was she so perverted?

She showed Toivo her sketches, drawn from memory some two hours after the panic. Oleg and she set up camp in some empty house in Sula, and Oleg first tried to give her tonic and help her recover with psychomassage, but nothing helped, and then she grabbed a sheet of paper, some disgusting stylus, hard and bent, and began hurriedly, one line after another, shadow by shadow, reproducing on paper the nightmare in her mind that blurred the real world.

The drawings looked unremarkable. A tangled web of lines, some familiar items—railings, a table, hedges—and over it all, indistinct shapes casting blurry shadows. Still, the drawings did produce some feelings of anxiety, inappropriateness, and discomfort. Oleg Olegovich thought that there was something to the drawings but that reality had been much simpler and more disgusting, but he was no man of art. An unqualified consumer of it, no more than that.

He asked Toivo what had been discovered. Toivo presented his suppositions: Fleming, Nizhnyaya Pesha, a new type of embryophore, and so on. Oleg Pankratov nodded in agreement and then remarked with some sadness that the most disappointing part to him was . . . How to put it? Let's say, how skittish modern-day earthlings are. Everyone ran away, all of them! If only someone would show curiosity and interest . . . Here Toivo stepped in to defend the honor of modern earthlings and recounted the stories of Albina and Kir.

Oleg Olegovich was thrilled and jubilant. He slapped the armrests and the table with his spade-like hands; he gave Toivo and Zosya victorious looks and exclaimed, laughing, "That's my boy Kir! What a fellow! I've always said he'd turn out great . . . And our Albina! So much for all the would-you-kindlies and my-honored-neighbors!" Zosya fervently announced that it was unsurprising, that old and young were cast of the same mold. "And don't forget space explorers," Oleg Olegovich exclaimed.

"Don't forget space explorers, my love dove!" They argued, half joking and half serious, when a minor incident occurred.

Oleg Olegovich, grinning from ear to ear as his love dove talked, suddenly stopped grinning, and the joy on his face gave way to confusion, as if he had just been shaken to his core by something. Toivo followed his look and was treated to the sight of cottage number seven, door ajar and an inconsolable, disappointed Ernst Jürgen leaning on it, now in a simple beige suit instead of the craycrab fisherman's contraption. In one hand he held a beer can, and in the other an enormous sandwich with some reddish-white mystery, and he took turns chewing, drinking, and swallowing from one hand and then the other, eyes fixed on the clubhouse doors.

"But there's Ernst!" Zosya exclaimed, "and you were saying!"

"Well, I'll be . . ." Oleg Olegovich uttered slowly, with the same look of utter puzzlement.

"As you see, Ernst did not get scared either," sneered Zosya.

"I do see," Oleg Olegovich agreed.

He did know something about this Ernst Jürgen, and definitely didn't expect to see him here after yesterday's events. Ernst Jürgen had no business being here now, no business standing in his Malaya Pesha cottage, drinking beer and snacking on boiled craycrabs. Ernst Jürgen's business now should be hightailing it to Titan or beyond.

Toivo hurried to dispel the misunderstanding, explaining that Ernst Jürgen had not been in the village last night, and what Ernst Jürgen had in fact been doing last night was fishing for craycrabs upstream. Zosya was very saddened by the news, and Oleg Olegovich's relief was palpable. "Now I understand. You should have said so right away!" And even though nobody asked questions about his confusion, he started to explain himself: at night during the chaos he had surely seen Ernst Jürgen shamelessly elbowing himself a path to the null-T booth. Now he understands that it could not have happened, but at first, seeing Ernst Jürgen there with his beer, that was . . .

Zosya might have believed him; Toivo didn't believe a single word. There had been none of that, Oleg Olegovich did not see any Ernst Jürgens in the night, but he did know something else, something much more interesting about this Jürgen—evidently something unflattering if he was too shy to say it. And then a shadow fell on Malaya Pesha, the air filled with silky glocking sounds, and a worried Basil flew out from behind the clubhouse, putting on his overcoat as he ran, but sunlight had already returned to Malaya Pesha as a Puma-class pseudograv, shining gold like a giant bun, majestically landed on the square, not bending a single blade of grass, and this new, super-modern lander threw open its many oval portholes, out of which so many tall, tanned, purposeful, and loud figures emerged. They scattered, dragging some kind of boxes with sockets, carrying hoses with the oddest nozzles, lighting their blitzconnectors, fussing, running, waving—and none of them fussed, ran, waved, dragged, and carried more than Leo Duremar Tolstov, clothes still covered in dried green seaweed.

OFFICE OF THE DIRECTOR OF UNCONVENTIONAL EVENTS, MAY 6, '99, ABOUT ONE IN THE AFTERNOON

"And what did they achieve with all their tech?" I asked.

Toivo stared out of the window, bored, his eyes following Cloud City, which was now drifting somewhere above southern Sverdlovsk.

"Nothing substantially new," he replied. "They reconstructed the likely appearance of the animals. Got the same test results as the emergency crews. They were amazed by the lack of embryophore shells. Were perplexed by the energetics, kept saying it was impossible."

"Have you sent inquiries?" I forced myself to ask.

I have to emphasize again that by then I could see, know, and understand everything, but had no clue what to do with all of my seeing, knowing, and understanding. I could not come up with anything, and my employees were only making it worse. Toivo Glumov in particular.

My greatest desire was to send him on a vacation right there and then. Send them all on vacation, to the last intern, then turn off all communications, lower the shields, close my eyes, and spend a day, at least, completely alone. Not thinking about my facial expressions. Not worrying about which words sound natural and which sound off. Not thinking about anything at all, letting an empty void appear in my mind, and then the solution would present itself in that void. It was like a hallucination, of the kind you get when dealing with constant pain. I had been dealing with it for five weeks already, my mental reserves were nearing their end, but I could still control my face, control my behavior, and ask sensible questions.

"You sent inquiries?" I asked Toivo Glumov.

"I sent inquiries," he replied in a flat voice. "To Bürgermeier of Embryomechanics Cooperative. To Gorbatskoy, his eyes only. And to Fleming. Just in case. All in your name."

"All right," I said, "Let us wait."

Now I had to let him speak his mind. I could see that he needed to speak. To make sure that his superiors haven't missed the main point. Ideally, the superior should himself summarize the main point, but I had no strength left for that.

"Would you like to add something?" I asked.

"Yes. I do." He flicked an invisible speck of dust off the desk. "The unusual technology isn't the main point. The main point is the disparity of reactions."

"Meaning?" I asked. (Still I had to encourage him!)

"You could note that the events divided witnesses into two unequal groups. Even three, strictly speaking. The majority of witnesses were consumed by complete panic. The devil in a medieval village. Total loss of self-control. People weren't just fleeing Malaya Pesha, they were fleeing Earth. Now, group two—the zootechnician Anatoly Sergeyevich and the painter Zosya Lyadova, who got frightened initially but later found the courage to return, and the painter even saw something beautiful in those animals. And finally, the old ballerina and the boy Kir. And, I suppose, the space explorer Pankratov, Lyadova's husband. They never experienced fear—rather the opposite. Disparity of reactions," he repeated.

I knew what he was expecting me to do. All the conclusions were in plain sight. Somebody had performed a natural selection experiment in Malaya Pesha, dividing people by their reactions into those who were fit for something and those who weren't. Just like this someone performed selection in subspace entry sector 41/02. And there was no question of who this was that possessed technology well beyond ours. It was the same entity that for some reason saw fukamization as an obstacle. Toivo Glumov could have expressed all of that himself, but in his view that would have been a violation of professional ethics and filial piety.

Such conclusions were for the superiors and the clan's elders to make.

I did not exercise the prerogative. It was too much for me. "Disparity," I repeated. "Very convincing."

That probably sounded fake, because Toivo suddenly lifted his long white eyelashes and stared right at me.

"Was that all?" I immediately asked.

"Yes, that's all."

"All right. Let's wait for the lab results. What are you going to do now? Sleep?"

He sighed almost imperceptibly. "The superiors didn't consider it necessary to . . ." Here a less composed man would have said something insolent. Toivo said, "I don't know. I'll go work some more, I think. The count should be done today."

"The whales?"

"Yes."

"Fine," I said, "as you wish. But tomorrow, kindly go to Kharkov."

Toivo raised his fair eyebrows but said nothing.

"Do you know what the Oddball Institute is?" I asked.

"Yes. Kikin told me."

My turn to raise eyebrows. Mentally. Damn them all, they've really loosened up. Do I really have to tell everyone every time to keep their mouths shut? Like this is some gossip club, not COMCON-2.

"And what did Kikin tell you?" I asked.

"It's a branch of the Institute for Metapsychic Studies. They're studying the extremes of the human psyche and beyond. Lots of strange people there."

"That's right," I said. "You're going there tomorrow. Here's your task."

I expressed the task as follows. On March 25, the Oddball Institute in Kharkov had the honor of receiving the famous Sorcerer from the planet of Saraksh. Who is Sorcerer? He is, of course, a mutant. Moreover, he's the king and ruler of all the mutants in the radioactive jungle beyond the Blue Serpent. He has many wondrous abilities; in particular he's a psychocrat. What's a psychocrat? It's a general term for any creature that can exert control over other minds. In addition, Sorcerer is a creature of immense intellect, one of the rare sapiens who can infer the existence of oceans from a drop of water. Sorcerer came to Earth in his private capacity. For some reason, his main interest was the Oddball Institute. Maybe he was looking for others like him, we don't know. He was scheduled to stay for four days but left after one hour. Returned to Saraksh and vanished into his radioactive jungle.

Up to that point, my summary had been the truth and nothing but the truth. Then the misferences began.

Our progressors on Saraksh have been trying to contact Sorcerer for a month now, by my request. They have had no success. Maybe we offended Sorcerer here on Earth somehow and were none the wiser. Maybe one hour was enough for him to collect all the information he needed. Or maybe it was something very Sorcerery and therefore unimaginable to us. In any case, the task is to go to the Institute, look through any documentation regarding Sorcerer's examination (if one was conducted), talk to all employees that interacted with him, find out whether something strange had happened during Sorcerer's visit, if he said something notable about the Earth and us humans, if he did something that seemed insignificant but could now be seen in a different light.

"Understood?" I asked.

He shot me another quick look. "You never said what subject this trip falls under."

No, it was not a flash of intuition. And I don't think he had caught my misferences. He was genuinely unable to understand how his superior, now in possession of such important information about the insidious work of the hated Wanderers, could have something unrelated on his mind.

And I said, "Same subject. 'The Visit of the Old Lady.'" (That was in fact true. In a broad sense. The very broadest.)

He sat silent for a while, noiselessly tapping his fingers on the desk. Then he spoke, as if apologizing: "I don't see how it relates . . ."

"You will," I promised.

He was quiet.

"And if there is no relation, it's for the better," I said. "He's a sorcerer, understand? A real sorcerer, I know him. A real fairy tale sorcerer, with a talking bird on his shoulder and all other trappings. And a sorcerer from another planet on top of it. I need him badly!"

"A possible ally," Toivo said, his tone weakly questioning.

Well then, he found his explanation. He will work with frenzy now. Maybe he'll even find Sorcerer. Though very doubtful.

"Keep in mind," I said, "in Kharkov you'll be an employee of the first COMCON. This isn't a cover story; the first COMCON really is looking for Sorcerer."

"All right," he said.

"Is that all? Then go. Go, go. Greetings to Asya."

He left, and I was finally alone. For a few blissful minutes. Until the next videophone call. And it was during those minutes of bliss I decided I had to go to see Athos. See him immediately, because when he's getting his surgery, there will not be a single person I can go to.

DOCUMENT 5

To: COMCON-2, Sverdlovsk, M. Kammerer
From: Gorbatskoy, Director of TPO Biocenter

In response to your query on May 6.
You are being fooled. That cannot be true. Forget it.
   Gorbatskoy

(END OF DOCUMENT 5)

DOCUMENT 6

To: COMCON-2, Kammerer
From: Fleming

Maxim!
I know all about the event in Malaya Pesha. An unbelievable case in my opinion, I'm envious. Your guys were very exact in their questions to us. I'm working on it, top priority. I'll let you know as soon as something becomes clear.
    Fleming
    Nizh. Pesha, 3:30 PM.

P.S.: Or maybe you know something through your channels by now? If so, let me know immediately! I'm in Nizhnyaya Pesha for the next three days.

P.P.S.: Could it really be the Wanderers? Damn, would that be exciting!

(END OF DOCUMENT 6)

DOCUMENT 7

From: Embryomechanics Production Cooperative, Directorate
  Earth, Antarctic Region, Erebus
  A 18/03, 62; O/T Index KC 946239; Comms SKC-76
  Adolf Anna Bürgermeier, General Director
  S-283, May 7, '99
To: COMCON-2, Ural-North, UE
  Comms SRZ-23
  Director M. Kammerer
Contents: Response to your query on May 6, '99

Dear Kammerer!
With regards to the properties of modern embryophores that are
of interest to you, I can relay the following.

1. The total mass of created biomechanisms is up to 200 kg. The maximum number of them is eight. The maximum size of an individual
can be determined by the program 102-ASTA $(M, \rho, \rho0, k)$, where M is
the mass of the source material, ρ is the density of the source material,
$\rho0$ is the density of the environment, and k is the number of mecha-
nisms being developed. The calculation is highly accurate for temperatures in the 200–400 K range with a pressure within 0–200 atm.

2. An embryophore's development time is a variable dependent
on many parameters that are fully controlled by the initiator. For
the fastest-developing embryophores, there exists a lower value
of approximately 1 minute.

3. The lifespan of currently known biomechanisms depends on
their individual mass. A biomechanism's critical mass M_0 equals
12 kg. Biomechanisms with mass M that does not exceed M_0 have

a theoretically infinite lifespan. The lifespan of biomechanisms with mass above M_0 decreases exponentially with the excess mass, so the lifespan of the most massive ones (on the order of 100 kg) cannot exceed a few seconds.

4. Creation of a fully dissipating embryophore has long been a research interest but remains far from solved. Current state-of-the-art technology cannot produce shells that would be fully governed by the life cycle.

5. Microscopic biomechanisms are highly mobile (covering a distance up to 1,000 times their size per minute). As for field variants, the current record is the KS-3 Bouncer model, capable of stimulated directional movement at speeds up to 5 m/s.

6. It is fully certain that any currently viable biomechanism has an intense and clearly negative reaction to natural biofields. This is part of any biomechanism's genetic system, and not out of ethical considerations, as many assume, but because any natural biofield of intensity above 0.63 GD (a kitten's biofield) critically disrupts the biomechanism's signaling network.

7. Regarding energy balance. An embryophore releasing biomechanisms with parameters that you described in your query would undoubtedly lead to a rapid release of energy (an explosion), if the situation you described were possible at all. It follows from the previous points, however, that the situation appears entirely fantastic given the current level of scientific and technological development.

Respectfully yours,
General Director Bürgermeier

(END OF DOCUMENT 7)

DOCUMENT 8

COMCON-2, Ural-North.

Report 016/99

Date: May 8, '99

Author: Inspector T. Glumov

Subject: 009, "The Visit of the Old Lady"

Contents: Concerning the stay by Sorcerer (Saraksh) at the Kharkov branch of the Institute for Metapsychic Studies (Oddball Institute)

According to my orders, I arrived at the Kharkov branch of the Oddball Institute yesterday morning. Branch deputy director Logovenko scheduled a meeting with me for 10:00 AM; however, I was not allowed into his office directly. I was first examined in an oscillating frequency chamber OFC-8, also known as the Oddball Finder Contraption. It turned out that every new visitor to the branch undergoes this procedure. Its goal is to screen random people for "latent metapsychic abilities," or in other words to find "hidden oddballs."

At 10:25, I introduced myself to the deputy director for relations with public organizations.

(Daniel Alexandrovich Logovenko, doctor of psychology, corresponding member of the European Academy of Medical Sciences. Born 09/17/30 in Borispol. Education: Institute of Psychology, Kiev; management faculty, Kiev University; special course in advanced and anomalous ethology, Split. His main research achievements are in the field of metapsychology—discovery of the so-called "Logovenko impulse," also knows as the "T wave mentogram." One of the founders of the Kharkov branch of the Institute for Metapsychic Studies.)

D. Logovenko told me that he had personally met Sorcerer at the Mirzachirla spaceport on March 25 and accompanied him to the Institute. Also present were the branch's section chief Bohdan Haidai and Sorcerer's escort from COMCON-1, Borya Laptev, whom we know well.

Upon arriving at the branch, Sorcerer evaded the traditional preliminary conversation with refreshments and expressed his desire to immediately start familiarizing himself with the work and the clientele of the organization. Then D. Logovenko handed Sorcerer over to B. Haidai and had no further interactions with Sorcerer.

> ME: What do you think Sorcerer's goal was in visiting the Institute?
>
> LOGOVENKO: Sorcerer told me nothing about that. COMCON told us that Sorcerer was supposedly interested in our work, and we were happy to let him learn about it. Not purely out of kindness; we had hoped to examine him as well. We have never encountered a psychocrat of such power, and an alien to boot.
>
> ME: What did the examination show?
>
> LOGOVENKO: The examination was not conducted. Sorcerer cut his visit short, to everyone's complete surprise.
>
> ME: Why do you think that happened?
>
> LOGOVENKO: We're all at a loss here. Here's what I'm inclined to guess. He was introduced to Michel Desmond, a polymental. And Sorcerer possibly saw in Michel something that we had missed but that frightened him, or insulted— shocked him so much that he lost the desire to talk to us. Don't forget that he is a psychocrat, an intellectual, yes, but by origin, by upbringing, you could even say by worldview, he's a typical savage.
>
> ME: I do not quite understand. What is a polymental?
>
> LOGOVENKO: Polymentalism is an exceedingly rare metapsychic phenomenon, the coexistence of two or more individual consciousnesses in one human body. Don't confuse it with schizophrenia—it's not a pathology. Take our Michel

Desmond. He's a perfectly healthy, very pleasant young man with no deviations. But a decade ago it was noted, by sheer chance, that he has a double mentogram. One is a perfectly ordinary human mentogram, clearly tied to Michel's past and present life. And another, only visible at a specific depth during mentoscopy. That mentogram belongs to a creature that has nothing in common with Michel, living in a world that we have not been able to identify. It seems to be a world of unusually high pressure and high temperatures . . . but that is beside the point. The point is that Michel has no conception of that world, or of this second consciousnesses, while that creature has no conception of Michel or our world. So I'm thinking that we discovered one such neighbor consciousness in Michel, but maybe there are more in him, beyond our instruments, and they shocked Sorcerer.

ME: Doesn't this Desmond's other world shock you?

LOGOVENKO: I know what you mean. No, it doesn't. Certainly not. But I have to say, the mentoscopist who first looked into that world experienced a severe shock. Mainly, of course, because he decided Michel must be some kind of Wanderer infiltrator, a progressor from another world.

ME: How was that established not to be the case?

LOGOVENKO: We're safe in that regard. Michel's behavior has no correlation to the functioning of the other consciousness. A polymental's neighboring consciousnesses do not interact in any way. They cannot interact in principle—they operate in different spaces. By the way of a crude analogy, imagine shadow puppetry. The shadows on the screen cannot interact. Of course some entirely fantastical suppositions remain, but they're just that, fantastical.

That concluded my conversation with D. Logovenko, and I was introduced to B. A. Haidai.

(Bohdan Arkhipovich Haidai, master's degree in psychology. Born 06/10/55 in Seredyna-Buda. Education: Institute of Psychology, Kiev; special course in advanced and anomalous ethology,

Split. Main research achievements are in the field of metapsychology. Employed by the psychoforecasting division since '89, chief of the technical support laboratory since '93, chief of the intrapsychic technology section since '94.)

A fragment of our conversation:

ME: What do you think Sorcerer's main interest was here at the Institute?

HAIDAI: You know, I'm thinking this Sorcerer was misinformed. That is not surprising. Even here on Earth, many have the wrong idea about our work, so what could you expect from progressors that Sorcerer dealt with on Saraksh? I was surprised right away that Sorcerer, an alien, wanted to see our institute and only it of all the places on Earth. I'm thinking, here's the thing: At home on Saraksh, he's the king of mutants, so to speak, and probably has a lot of trouble because of that. They grow weak, they get sick, they have to be treated and supported somehow. And our oddballs here are also sort of like mutants, so he had probably imagined we would have useful information here, that the Institute was something like a clinic.

ME: And, realizing the misunderstanding, he just turned and left?

HAIDAI: Exactly. Turned too sharply maybe, left too hurriedly, but for all we know that's the manners they have over there.

ME: What did he talk to you about?

HAIDAI: He didn't talk to me about anything. I only heard his voice once. I asked him what he would like to see here and he said, "Everything you will show." His voice is quite unpleasant, I have to say, like a grumpy witch's.

ME: By the way, what language did you converse in?

HAIDAI: Ukrainian, imagine that!

Haidai testified that Sorcerer met only three clients of the Institute. I have so far managed to speak to two of them.

Marina Sergeyevna Ravich, twenty-seven years old, veterinarian by training, currently a consultant at the Leningrad Embryosystems Plant, the Lausanne Workshop on P-Abstraction Realizations, the Belgrade Institute of Laminar Positronics and the Yakutsk Region Chief Architect's Office. A timid, very shy, and sad woman. She has a unique and unexplained ability (it hasn't even been named scientifically yet). If she is presented with a clearly defined problem that she understands, she starts solving it with passion and joy, but in the end, completely against her will, she finds the solution to some other problem that has nothing in common with the one at hand, usually something outside of her areas of professional interest. The problem she is presented with acts like a catalyst for her mind, causing it to solve some other problem that she had briefly read about in a pop-science magazine or had overheard some experts discussing. Determining which problem she is going to solve in advance seems to be entirely impossible, akin to the uncertainty principle of quantum physics. Sorcerer walked into her office as she was working. She vaguely remembers an ugly, big-headed figure wrapped in green, and that is her only impression of Sorcerer. No, he did not say anything. Bohdan was saying the usual well-meaning stupidities about her ability, and that's the only voice she remembers. Haidai says Sorcerer only spent two minutes with her, so it seems like she was as uninteresting to him as he was to her.

Michel Desmond, forty-one years old, granular engineer by training, professional athlete, European tunnel hockey champion of '88. A jovial man, happy with himself and with the universe. Treats his polymentalism humorously and with indifference. He was about to go to the stadium when Sorcerer arrived. Sorcerer, according to him, looked sickly and was silent, didn't get any jokes; he seemed not to understand where he was and what people were saying. There was a brief moment—Michel will remember it until his dying hour—when Sorcerer lifted his long pale eyelids and stared straight into Michel's soul, or maybe deeper, into the very world in which the creature Michel shares

his mental space with lives. It was an unpleasant but also wondrous moment. Shortly after that, Sorcerer left, without opening
his mouth. Or saying good-bye.

Susumu Hirota, also known as Senrigan, meaning "seeing for
a thousand miles." Eighty-three years old, a historian of religion,
a professor of religious history at Bangkok University. I did not
manage to see him; he will only be back at the Institute in a day
or two. Haidai thinks Sorcerer strongly disliked this clairvoyant.
In any case, Sorcerer made his exit during their meeting.

According to all the witnesses, the exit went like this: Sorcerer was standing in the middle of a mentoscopy room, listening
to Haidai's lecture on Senrigan's unusual abilities, with Senrigan
occasionally interrupting to reveal yet another private detail about
Haidai, and then suddenly, without saying a word, with no warning look or gesture, this green gnome sharply turned, elbowing
Borya Laptev, and quickly walked through the corridors to the
exit, without pausing anywhere for a second. And it was over.

A few more people at the Kharkov branch had seen Sorcerer—junior researchers, lab techs, a few of the administrative
staff. None of them knew who he was. And only two, newcomers
to the Institute, paid Sorcerer any attention, struck by his appearance. I got no useful information out of them.

Then I met with Borya Laptev. The most relevant part of our
conversation follows:

ME: You're the only one who was with Sorcerer all the way,
from Saraksh and back to Saraksh. Did you notice anything
strange about him?
BORIS: That's some question! You know, it's like when a camel
was asked, why is your neck crooked? And the camel said,
but what part of me is straight?
ME: Even so? Try to think about his recent behavior. Something must have happened for him to act out like that.
BORIS: Look, I've known Sorcerer for two of our years. He is an
inexhaustible creature. I've long given up on even trying to
understand him. What can I tell you? He had a depressive

episode on that day, as I call it. He has those sometimes for no obvious reason. Becomes very quiet, and if he opens his mouth it's only to say something nasty, some obnoxious remark. That was one of those days. We were flying from Saraksh and he was great, coining aphorisms, joking at my expense, even singing. But then at Mirzachirla he became grim, barely even talked to Logovenko, and then, when we went through the Institute with Haidai, he got gloomier than a storm. I was getting concerned that he was just about to insult someone, but then he must have realized himself that he couldn't carry on like that, so he got out of harm's way. And then was silent all the way to Saraksh. Only in Mirzachirla, he took a look around, as if in farewell, and squeaked in an annoying, whiny voice, "He sees the hills and sees the skies, but misses all that closer lies."

ME: What does that mean?

BORIS: Some children's rhyme. Ancient.

ME: How did you interpret it?

BORIS: I interpreted it not at all. I saw he was angry at the whole world, so I'd better keep silent before he bites me. So we flew to Saraksh in silence.

ME: And that's it?

BORIS: That's it. Just before landing, he mumbled some nonsense again: "Let's wait for the blind to see the seeing." We made it to the Blue Serpent. He gave a wave and, as you say it, disappeared into the jungle. No *thank you*, no *come visit*.

ME: Can you say anything more?

BORIS: What do you want from me? Yes, he really disliked something he saw here on Earth. What that was, well, he didn't deign to share. I'm telling you, he is a creature unpredictable beyond comprehension. Maybe the Earth had nothing to do with it. Maybe he just had a stomachache—in the broad sense, of course, very broad, cosmically—

ME: Do you think it's a coincidence, a rhyme about missing something, then about the blind and the seeing?

BORIS: That thing with the blind and the seeing, they have a saying in Pandeia, on Saraksh, "When the blind can see the seeing." It's like "When pigs fly," or "Not in a month of Sundays." He was saying something would never happen. The rhyme was just him being obnoxious. He obviously said it to mock someone, I just don't know whom. Maybe that bragging Japanese bore.

PRELIMINARY CONCLUSIONS

1. I made no discoveries that could help in locating Sorcerer on Saraksh.
2. I can make no further recommendations regarding continuing the search.

T. Glumov

(END OF DOCUMENT 8)

✦✦✦

On the evening of May 6, our president, Athos-Sidorov, saw me. I took the most interesting materials with me, and verbally relayed my summary and recommendations. He was very ill, his face sallow, his breathing troubled. I had waited too long for this meeting; he wasn't even well enough to truly feel surprise. He said he would study the materials, give them some thought, and contact me the next day.

On May 7, I spent the entire day in my office waiting for his call. He never called. In the evening I got word that he had suffered a very serious episode and was in the hospital, barely resuscitated. Once again everything fell to me alone, the very bones of my soul cracking under all that weight.

On May 8, I received, among other things, Toivo's report on his Oddball Institute visit. I ticked his name off my list, entered his report into the registrator and began coming up with an assignment for Petya Siletsky. By then, only Petya Siletsky and Zoya Morozova had not yet visited the Institute.

At approximately the same time, Toivo Glumov was in his work office, talking to Grisha Serosovin. Below I offer a reconstruction of their conversation, mainly in order to illustrate the mindset that my employees had at the time. Only in terms of quality. The quantity was still the same: Toivo Glumov alone on one side, and everyone else on the other.

UNCONVENTIONAL EVENTS DEPARTMENT, OFFICE D, MAY 8, '99 , EVENING

Grisha Serosovin entered with no knock as usual, stopped in the doorway, and asked, "May I?"

Toivo put *Vertical Progress* by the anonymous K. Oxoview aside and lowered his head to study Grisha. "Please. But I'm going home soon."

"Sandro's not here again?"

Toivo looked at Sandro's desk. It was empty and spotless. "Yes. Three days now."

Grisha sat behind Sandro's desk and crossed his legs. "And where did you vanish to yesterday?" he asked.

"Kharkov."

"Oh, so you've also been to Kharkov now?"

"Who else has?"

"Just about everyone. Nearly the whole department has been to Kharkov in the last month. Look, Toivo, why I dropped by here: You've dealt with the cases of sudden genius, right?"

"Yes, but a long time ago. Two years."

"Remember Soddy?"

"I do, Bartholomew Soddy. A mathematician turned confessor."

"Yes, right, him," Grisha said. "There was a sentence in the case file. I'm quoting, 'According to the existing information, B. Soddy experienced a personal tragedy not long before the transformation.' If you wrote the file, two questions: What was the tragedy, and where did you get the information?"

Toivo moved his hand to the terminal, calling up his program. It had finished information collection and was already calculating. Toivo began cleaning his desk with deliberate movements. Grisha waited patiently. Not for the first time.

"If it says 'According to the existing information,'" Toivo said, "it means the information came from Big Bug."

He fell silent. Grisha waited some more, shifted his crossed legs and spoke: "I don't want to trouble Big Bug with that detail. Fine, I'll try to manage . . . Listen, Toivo, don't you think our Big Bug has been jumpy lately?"

Toivo shrugged. "Maybe," he said. "The president is really doing bad. Gorbovsky is on his deathbed, they say. And he knows them all. Knows them well."

Grisha pondered. "By the way, I also know Gorbovsky, if you can believe it. Remember . . . no, you were not here then . . . Kamill committed suicide. The last of the Devil's Dozen. Then again, the Devil's Dozen is of course just a name to you. I had never heard about it back then. This unfortunate Kamill's suicide, or rather self-destruction, was itself clear. But the why was unclear. Of course, he led a sorrowful life, he had been completely alone for the last century . . . lonelier than we can even imagine . . . but I'm not talking about that. Big Bug sent me to see Gorbovsky then, because as it turns out, Gorbovsky once knew this Kamill well, and even tried to befriend him . . . Are you listening to me?"

Toivo nodded several times. "I am."

"Do you know what you look like?"

"I do," Toivo said. "Like a person lost in their own thoughts. You've told me that. Several times. A cliché. Agreed?"

Instead of replying, Grisha suddenly grabbed a stylus from his shirt pocket and threw it straight at Toivo's head, like a dart across the room. Toivo plucked the stylus of the air with two fingers, inches from his face.

"Weak," he said.

WEAK, he wrote with the same stylus on a paper in front of him.

"You're pitying me, good sir," Toivo voiced, "and you shouldn't. It isn't good for me."

"You know, Toivo," Grisha spoke emotionally, "I'm sure your reflexes are good. Not excellent, no, but good, a decent professional's reflexes. But the way you look . . . as your subacc coach, it is my duty to occasionally check if you can react to your surroundings, or if you're really cataleptic . . ."

"I'm tired today," Toivo said. "The program will be done now, and I'll go home."

"What do you have there in the program?" Grisha asked.

HAVE THERE, Toivo wrote on the paper, and said, "I have whales there. I have birds there. I have lemmings, rats, voles. I have many of our lesser friends."

"And what are they doing in the program?"

"They are perishing. Or fleeing. They die, beaching themselves, drowning themselves, flying away from where they lived for centuries."

"Why?"

"Nobody knows. Two or three centuries ago that was common, even though they didn't understand why. Then, for a long time, nothing like that happened. At all. And now it's started again."

"Sorry," Grisha said. "This is of course highly interesting, but what do we have to do with it?"

Toivo sat silent. Not getting an answer, Grisha asked, "You think it could have something to do with the Wanderers?"

Toivo was laboriously studying the stylus, turning it in his fingers, even taking it by the tip and holding it up to the light. "Anything we cannot explain could have to do with the Wanderers."

"Very succinct," Grisha said with admiration.

"Or could have nothing to do with them," Toivo added. "Where do you get such beautiful items? Just a stylus, you might think. What could be more mundane? But yours is pleasant to look at. You know, you can give it to me as a gift. And I will gift it to Asya. I want to make her happy. With something at least."

"And I would make you happy with something," Grisha said.

"And you would make me happy with something."

"Keep it," Grisha said, "own it. Gift it, present it, make some-thing up. How you designed it and spent nights shaping it."

"Thank you," Toivo said, putting the stylus into his pocket.

"Keep in mind, though"—Grisha raised a finger—"Here on Red Maple Street, just around the corner, there's a machine from one F. Moran's workshop that prints such styli as fast as you can press the button."

Toivo pulled the stylus out again and studied it. "In any case," he said sadly, "you noticed the machine on Red Maple Street; the thought would never have crossed my mind . . ."

"But you noticed something wrong in the whale world!" Grisha said.

WHALES, Toivo wrote on the sheet.

"Speaking of," he said, "you're new to this, no prejudices, so what do you think? What does it take for a pod of whales—tamed, fed, loved—to suddenly, like centuries ago, in vicious ancient times, throw themselves onto a sandbar and die? Silently, without calling for help, with their young . . . can you imagine any reason for such suicides?"

"Why did they do that in the old times?"

"Why they did so centuries ago, we don't know that either. But at least there are reasonable guesses. Whales were tortured by parasites, whales were attacked by orcas and squids, whales were attacked by people . . . Some even imagined they were com-mitting suicide in protest. But today!"

"And what do the experts say?"

"The experts requested that COMCON-2 uncover the reason for renewed suicides of cetaceans."

"Hmm, I see . . . and what do the herders say?"

"The herders are where it all started. The herders say that whales are committing suicide out of sheer horror. And the herders do not understand, cannot even imagine, what modern whales could be afraid of."

"Uh-huh," Grisha said. "It really looks like the Wanderers had a hand in that."

HAD A HAND, Toivo wrote, then framed the words, drew another frame, and started shading the area between the lines.

"But then again," Grisha continued, "all of this has happened before, again and again. We're guessing wildly here, blaming the Wanderers, twisting our brains, and then one day, Oh! Who is that familiar figure on the horizon? Who is it here, so graceful, proudly smiling like the Lord himself on the sixth day of creation? Whose snow-white goatee is it that's so familiar? Mister Fleming, sir! How did you come to be here, sir? Would you kindly follow us, sir, to the courtroom? To the World Council, Emergency Tribunal!"

"You have to admit, that would be far from the worst resolution," Toivo remarked.

"But of course! Although sometimes I think I'd rather deal with a dozen Wanderers than with one Fleming. That could be because the Wanderers are almost hypothetical, and Fleming with his goatee is a real creature. Discouragingly real, with his snow-white goatee, his Nizhnyaya Pesha, his lab thugs, his goddamn fame!"

"I see you particularly object to the goatee."

"I don't mind the goatee," Grisha argued sarcastically. "We could go grab him by that goatee. But what are we going to grab the Wanderers by, if it turns out to be them?"

Toivo carefully slid the stylus into his pocket, rose, and stood by the window. Out of the corner of his eye, he could see Grisha watching him carefully, legs uncrossed and even bending forward. It was quiet; only the terminal was beeping softly as calculations flowed on the screen.

"Or are you hoping it's not them?" Grisha asked.

Toivo didn't reply for a while, then responded without turning: "I'm not, not anymore."

"Meaning?"

"It's them."

Grisha squinted. "Meaning?"

Toivo turned to face him. "I'm convinced that the Wanderers are on Earth, and they're active."

(Grisha later recounted that the moment was a very unpleasant shock. He felt like he wasn't in reality. It had everything to do with Toivo Glumov's personality: the words Toivo Glumov said were very hard to reconcile with Toivo Glumov the person. The words couldn't be a joke, because Toivo never joked about the Wanderers. The words couldn't be a rash conclusion, because Toivo never made rash conclusions. And the words could not be the truth, because they could not possibly be the truth. Then again, Toivo could be mistaken . . .)

Grisha asked in a tense voice, "Does Big Bug know?"

"I reported all the facts to him."

"And then?"

"So far, as you see, nothing," Toivo said.

Grisha relaxed and leaned back in his chair. "You're just mistaken," he said in relief.

Toivo said nothing.

"Damn you!" Grisha suddenly exclaimed. "You and all your gloomy fantasies! This was like a bucket of cold water!"

Toivo said nothing. He was looking out the window again. Grisha croaked, grabbed the tip of his nose, and, flinching, made circular motions with it. "No," he said, "I cannot be like you, that's the thing. I cannot. This is too serious. This is against my basic premises. This isn't some private matter, where I can believe what I want, and you likewise. If I believed this, I must put all else aside, sacrifice all that I have, give everything up . . . take an oath, dammit! But our lives have many options! What's it like to pour it all into one thing? Sometimes I'm afraid and ashamed, and then I watch you with admiration . . . and sometimes, like right now, the sight of you angers me! Your self-torture, your martyr's obsession . . . and then I want to joke, to mock you, to laugh all your ideas off . . ."

"Listen," said Toivo, "what do you want from me?"

Grisha fell silent. "Indeed," he muttered. "What do I want from you? I don't know."

"I do. You want everything to be well, and better with every day."

"Oh!" Grisha raised a finger. He wanted to say something else, something to lighten the mood, to clear the awkward feeling of intimacy of the last few minutes, but then the computer program sounded completion, and a printout with results started falling onto the desk. Toivo looked through it, line by line, then carefully folded the printout and put it into the registrator.

"Nothing interesting?" Grisha asked with a measure of compassion.

"How do I put it," Toivo mumbled. Now he really was lost in thought. "Spring of '81 again."

"'Again' what?"

Toivo tapped on the terminal's sensors, running another program.

"In March of '81," he said, "the first mass suicide of gray whales in two hundred years was observed."

"Right," said Grisha impatiently, "so what's the 'again'?"

Toivo rose to his feet. "It's a long story," he said. "Read the summary report later. Let's head home."

TOIVO GLUMOV'S RESIDENCE, MAY 8, '99, LATE EVENING

They had dinner in a room painted crimson by the setting sun.

Asya was dismayed. The Pashkovsky fermentation starter, delivered to the delicacy factory straight from Pandora (in living biocontainer bags, covered in terra-cotta frost, bristling with evaporation hooks, thirteen pounds of precious starter per bag)—the starter had been acting up again. Its scent spontaneously degraded to sigma class, and its sourness was barely at the acceptable threshold. The expert council was in disagreement. The magister demanded to suspend all production of the alapies so beloved across the planet, while Bruno—the snot-nosed, insolent babbler—declared that no, why would they? He'd never dared to say a peep against the magister, but today was he was quite the orator. The typical consumer, he's sure, won't even notice such a subtle change of flavor, and the experts, he's sure, one in five at least, will be overjoyed at such variation—he'll bet his right arm on it . . . as if anyone needs his right arm. But the rest agreed with him! And now nobody knows what will happen . . .

Asya opened the window, sat on the sill, and looked down into the mile and a quarter of blue and green abyss below. "I'm afraid I might have to go to Pandora," she said.

"For a long time?" Toivo asked.

"I don't know. Could be long."

"And what for, exactly?" Toivo carefully asked.

"See, the thing is, the magister thinks that we've been through everything here on Earth. So something has to be wrong there, on the plantations. Maybe a new strain, or maybe something happens during transportation. We don't know."

"You already had to go to Pandora once." Toivo was getting grim. "Went for a week and spent three months there."

"Well, what do we do, then?"

Toivo scratched his cheek with a finger and grunted. "I don't know what to do. I do know that three months without you would be horrible."

"How about two years without me? When you were stuck on that . . . What was it . . . ."

"That you even mention it! That was ages ago! I was young, I was a fool . . . I was a progressor! A man of steel—muscles, mask, square jaw! Look, let your Sonya go instead. She's young, pretty, could find herself a husband there, eh?"

"Of course Sonya's coming as well. Any more ideas?"

"Yes. Let the magister go. He cooked this trouble up, so let him go solve it."

Asya just stared at him.

"I take my words back," Toivo said quickly. "A mistake. An oversight."

"He can't even leave Sverdlovsk! His taste buds! He hasn't been out of his district for a quarter century!"

"I'll remember," Toivo punctuated. "Forever. Won't happen again. I was as a fool, blithering, blathering, piffling. Let Bruno go."

Asya burned him with her indignant look for a few more seconds, then turned to look out the window again. "Bruno won't be going," she said angrily. "Bruno will now be dealing with his own new starter. He wants to stabilize and standardize it. We'll see about that." She shot Toivo a glance and laughed. "Look at you, sulking! 'Three months without you . . .'"

Toivo immediately rose, crossed the room, and sat on the floor at Asya's feet, resting his head against her knees.

"You need a vacation anyway," Asya said. "You could go hunting there. It's Pandora! Take a trip to the Dunes, see our plantations. You can't even imagine the sight of Pashkovsky plantations!"

Toivo squeezed his cheek harder against her knees, still silent. Then she also fell quiet, and neither spoke for a while, until Asya asked, "Is there something going on with you?"

"Why do you think that?"

"I don't know. I can see it."

Toivo sighed deeply, stood up, and also sat on the windowsill. "You see right," he said grimly. "There is. With me."

"What is it?"

Toivo squinted, looking at the black lines of clouds cutting across the coppery crimson blaze of the sunset. Glaucous-black forests clustering near the horizon. Thousand-floor skyscrapers making each district a bundle of thin black bars. The enormous metal dome of the Forum shining on the left, and the unbelievably flat surface of the round sea on the right. And black, squeaking swifts, darting out of the hanging gardens above only to disappear into the shrubbery of the block below.

"What's going on?" Asya asked.

"You're incredibly beautiful," Toivo said. "The voice of your eyes is deeper than all roses. I don't know what those words mean exactly, but they are about someone very beautiful. About you. You're more than just beautiful, you're splendid. A joy to look at. And your worries are so sweet. Your world is sweet. Even that Bruno of yours is sweet . . . The world is beautiful, if you must know. 'The world is pretty like a flower, with joy enough to fill five hearts, nine kidneys, and four livers . . .' I don't know what that verse is. It just came to mind, and I wanted to quote it . . . And I'll tell you this, remember! It might even be that I will soon join you on Pandora! Because his patience will run out soon enough and he'll kick me out on a vacation. Or just kick me out. I see it in his hazel eyes. Clearly, as if on a screen. And let's have tea now."

Asya stared at him with a penetrating gaze. "You're not getting anywhere, are you?" she asked.

Toivo avoided her eyes and gave an indecisive shrug.

"That's because you were thinking wrong from the start," Asya said passionately. "The task was wrong from the beginning! You cannot pose a question where any answer would disappoint you. Your hypothesis was faulty from the start, remember what I told you? If the Wanderers were really found, would you be happy? And now you're starting to understand that they're nowhere to be found, and you're miserable again—that you were wrong, you had an incorrect hypothesis, you feel like you lost without having lost anything."

"I've never argued against that," Toivo said abjectly. "I'm always at fault, such is my fate . . ."

"Look, and now he is also disappointed in this idea of yours . . . I of course don't believe that he would kick you out, you're talking nonsense, he loves and values you, everybody knows that . . . But really, you cannot waste so many years on . . . what exactly? Because you all have nothing, really, except an idea. Nobody's saying the idea is not interesting—it can make anyone nervous—but no more than that! It's essentially just an inverse of an old human practice . . . it's just the opposite of progressors. If we're trying to shape the history of others, then someone could be doing the same to us—No, wait, listen! First, you're forgetting that not everything has an opposite in reality. Grammar is one thing, reality is another. So at first it looked interesting, now it just looks . . . unseemly. Know what one of our people told me yesterday? He said, 'Well, we're not COMCONites, we can only envy them: when they encounter an impenetrable mystery, they quickly attribute it to the Wanderers and then they're done!'"

"Just who said that, I wonder?" Toivo grimly asked.

"What difference does it make? So our fermentation starter's gone mad. Why should we look for the cause? It's the Wanderers, of course! The bloody hand of the supercivilization! And don't get mad, please. Don't! So you don't like such jokes, but you almost never hear them. Just Sikorsky syndrome is trouble enough . . . and that's not a joke anymore. It's a sentence, my dears, a diagnosis!"

Toivo composed himself. "Well," he spoke, "you're on to something there about the starter. That's an unconventional event! Why didn't you report that?" he sternly asked. "Don't you know the rules? We'll go take the magister in!"

"You're some joker." Asya sounded angry. "Everyone's joking!"

"And that's great!" Toivo encouraged. "We should all be happy! When the real deal begins, you'll see, nobody will be joking—"

Asya slammed her little hand against her knee in frustration. "Oh God! Why don't you drop your act with me? You don't want to joke, you're not thinking of joking, and that's the worst about you all! You constructed this grim, dark world, a world of threats, fear, and suspicion . . . why? Where from? Where do you get this cosmic misanthropy?"

Toivo didn't respond.

"Maybe it's because your unexplained UEs are tragedies? But a UE is always a tragedy! Whether mysterious or plain to all, it's still a UE! Right?"

"Wrong," Toivo said.

"Are there ever any happy UEs?"

"Sometimes."

"Such as?" Asya asked, voice filling with venom.

"Let's have tea instead," Toivo offered.

"No, I'd rather hear you name a happy, joyful, uplifting unconventional event."

"Fine," Toivo said, "but then we're having tea. Agreed?"

"Oh, give me a break," Asya said.

They fell silent. Below, through the thick vegetation of the gardens, colored lights shone through the blue-tinted dusk. And the black skyscraper pillars sparkled in a cavalcade of lights.

"Do you know the name Goujon?" Toivo asked.

"Of course."

"And Soddy?"

"Naturally."

"What would you say is remarkable about those people?"

"What would I say? Anyone would say that Goujon is a brilliant composer and Soddy a remarkable confessor. What do you say?"

"And I say they're remarkable in another way entirely," Toivo said. "Albert Goujon was, until the age of fifty, a decent, but no more than that, agrophysicist with no musical talent whatsoever. The forty-year old Bartholomew Soddy was studying satellite shadow functions, and was known as a dry, pedantic loner. That is what makes those people remarkable, I would say."

"What do you mean by that? What's so remarkable about it? People with hidden talents, who worked long and hard, until quantity turned into quality."

"There was no quantity, Asya, that's the issue. Just the quality that suddenly changed. Radically. In an instant. Like an explosion."

Asya moved her lips silently, and then asked with hesitant sarcasm, "So you're saying what, the Wanderers inspired them, right?"

"I did not say that. You asked me to name some happy, uplifting UEs. Here you have some. I can name about a dozen more, although not as widely known."

"Fine. And why are you concerned with that exactly? What makes it your business?"

"Any unconventional event is our business."

"So I'm asking, what makes these events so unconventional?"

"They're unexplainable within our current framework of knowledge."

"There's plenty that is unexplainable in the world!" Asya exclaimed. "Readers are also unexplainable, but we're used to them."

"And we don't consider it unconventional if we're used to it. We don't deal with phenomena, Asya. We deal with specific occurrences, with events. Something that did not happen, had not happened for a thousand years, and then it suddenly happened.

Why did it happen? Unclear. How to explain it? The experts are scratching their heads. Then we start paying attention. See, Asya, you're classifying UEs incorrectly. We don't split them into happy and tragic ones, we split them into explained and unexplained."

"Are you really suggesting any unexplained UE is a threat?"

"Yes. Even a happy one."

"What threat could there possibly be in an ordinary agrophysicist's transformation into a musical genius?"

"I wasn't precise enough. The UE itself isn't the threat. The most mysterious UEs tend to be completely harmless. Sometimes even comical. It's the event's cause that can be a threat. The mechanism that created the UE. Because you could ask the question differently: Why did someone need to transform an agrophysicist into a musician?"

"Or maybe it was just a statistical fluke!"

"Maybe. The point is that we don't know. By the way, notice what you just arrived at . . . Tell me, please, how your explanation is better than ours. A statistical fluke, by definition unpredictable and uncontrollable, or the Wanderers, not much better, but you can at least in theory catch them. Sure, a statistical fluke sounds more serious, scientific, objective, unlike the same old vulgar, stupidly romantic, banally legendary—"

"Wait, don't get all sarcastic please," Asya said. "Nobody's denying your Wanderers. I am not quite saying that . . . You got me confused now, you always do! You confuse me, your Maxim, and then you go around sulking, would someone kindly console you! Yes, so what I wanted to say: Fine, assume the Wanderers really are interfering in our lives. That's not the argument. Why is it a bad thing, that's what I'm asking. Why do you make bogeymen out of them? I cannot understand. And nobody can! Why was it good when you were guiding the history of other worlds, but when someone tries to guide your history . . . Every child now knows that a superintelligence means goodness!"

"A superintelligence means supergoodness," Toivo said.

"So? Even better!"

"No," Toivo said, "not better at all. We know what goodness is, although not too clearly. Now what does supergoodness mean?"

Asya slammed her knees again. "I don't understand! Mindboggling! Where do you get this presumption of threat? Explain, spell it out!"

"You, all of you, are completely wrong about our assumptions." Toivo was getting angry. "Nobody believes that the Wanderers intend to do us harm. That is indeed extremely unlikely. It's something else that scares us! We're afraid that they will come and do good, as *they* understand it!"

"Good is always good!" Asya insisted.

"You know full well that is not so. Or maybe you really don't? But I've explained it to you. I spent only three years as a progressor, and with me I brought good, only good and nothing but good, and by heavens did they hate me, those people! And they had the right to. Because the gods had come without asking. Nobody called them, but they barged in and started doing good. The same good that is always good. And they did it in secret, because they knew right from the start that the mortals wouldn't understand their goals, or wouldn't accept even if they understood . . . This is the morally ethical structure of this damn situation! A feudal slave in Arkanar will not understand what communism is; a clever bourgeois three centuries later will understand and reject it in horror . . . these are the basics and yet we fail to apply them to ourselves. And why? Because we cannot imagine what the Wanderers can offer us. We fail to imagine the analogy! But I know two things. They came without asking, that's one. They came in secret, that's two. And that means, it implies, that they know better than us what we need, on the one hand, and they are sure that we will not understand or accept their goals on the other. I don't know about you, but I don't want that. I do *not* want that. That's it!" He said with finality. "And enough with this. I'm a tired, concerned, unkind man who shouldered an enormous responsibility. I have Sikorsky syndrome; I'm a psychopath and I suspect everyone.

I don't love anyone, I'm a monster, a sufferer, a monomaniac, I need to be protected, treated with compassion . . . You should tiptoe around me, kiss my shoulder, and tell me jokes . . . and tea! My God, will I not get any tea today?"

Without saying a word, Asya jumped down from the sill and went to make tea. Toivo lay down on the couch. Some exotic musical instrument was buzzing outside, just at the threshold of hearing. A giant butterfly flew in through the window, circled above the table, and sat on the visor screen, spreading its black patterned wings. Toivo reached for the service remote without rising, but his hand couldn't reach it.

Asya entered with a tray, poured tea into glasses, and sat next to him. "Look," Toivo whispered, indicating the butterfly with his gaze.

"Such a beauty," Asya whispered back.

"Maybe it would like to live here with us?"

"No, it wouldn't," Asya said.

"Why not? Remember, the Kazaryans had a dragonfly."

"It didn't live with them, it was an occasional visitor."

"So let her visit us. We can call her Martha."

"Why Martha?"

"What else?"

"Cynthia," said Asya.

"No," Toivo said decisively. "No Cynthias. It's Martha. Martha the Mayoress. And the screen can be the Major."

✦✦✦

I will not, of course, claim that they had this conversation, word for word, on the evening of May 8. But I know for certain that they talked a lot about these topics, argued, disagreed. I also know for certain that neither of them could convince the other.

Asya, of course, was unable to pass her eternal optimism on to her husband. Her optimism was fed by the very atmosphere surrounding her, the people she worked with, her kind and tasty job. Toivo was outside that optimistic world; his world was that of constant guardedness and alert, in which optimism passes from one person to another only rarely, under the best of circumstances, and not for long even then.

Toivo couldn't turn his wife into an accomplice, couldn't infect her with his foreboding of a coming threat. His arguments lacked specificity; they were too speculative, too imagined. They were part of a worldview that Asya saw no evidence for, a professional sickness of sorts. He failed to horrify Asya, to touch her with his revulsion, indignation, and enmity.

That is why, when the storm finally broke, they found themselves so unprepared and disconnected in its eye, as if they had never had their discussions, arguments, and passionate attempts to convince one another.

On the morning of May 9, Toivo went to Kharkov again to meet the clairvoyant Hirota and close the case of Sorcerer's visit.

DOCUMENT 9

COMCON-2, Ural-North
Report 017/99
Date: May 9, '99
Author: Inspector T. Glumov
Subject: 009, "The Visit of the Old Lady"
Contents: Addendum to report 016/99

Susumu Hirota, also known as Senrigan, saw me in his office at 10:45 AM. He is a short, well-built old man who looks much older than his age. Quite preoccupied with his "gift," and shows it off at every opportunity: your wife has problems at work . . . she will go to Pandora, don't hope otherwise . . . you got this stylus from a friend but forgot to give it to your wife . . . and so on in the same vein. Quite unpleasant, I have to say. Sorcerer's exodus, in his own words, happened thusly: "He probably got afraid that I was about to learn some innermost secret of his, and so he fled. He had no idea that I saw him as a blank whitish screen with no visible detail, because he's a creature of another world . . ."

T. Glumov.

(END OF DOCUMENT 9)

DOCUMENT 10

High priority!
COMCON-2, Ural-North
Report 018/99
Date: May 9, '99
Author: Inspector T. Glumov
Subject: 009, "The Visit of the Old Lady"
Contents: The Oddball Institute's interest in witnesses to Malaya
   Pesha events

During my conversation with the on-duty dispatcher at the Oddball Institute, on May 9 at 11:50 AM, the following event occurred.

During his conversation with me, the dispatcher Temirkanov was, at the same time, quickly and professionally taking data off the registrator and entering it into the computer's terminal. The entered data would show up on the display, and appeared in the format: surname, name and patronymic, age (presumably), geographic place name (place of birth? residence? work?), profession, some six-digit index.

I paid no attention to the display, until the following appeared:

KUBOTIEVA, ALBINA MILANOVNA
96, BALLERINA, ARKHANGEL'SK, 001507

Two names that mean nothing to me followed, and after that:

KOSTENETSKY, KIR
12, SCHOOLBOY, PETROZAVODSK, 001507

I remind you that these two people were witnesses to the events in Malaya Pesha; see my report 015/99 from 05/07.

It is likely that I lost composure for a few seconds, because Temirkanov asked what I was so surprised by. I improvised saying that Albina Kubotieva's name surprised me—she's a ballerina whom my parents, ardent ballet followers, told me a lot about, it's strange to see her name here, does Albina the Great also possess metapsychic talents? Temirkanov laughed and said that was a possibility. According to him, registrators at all Institute branches constantly receive information on people who could be of interest to metapsychologists. The majority of the information is from terminals at clinics, hospitals, wellness centers, and other medical institutions that have standard psychoanalyzers. The Kharkov branch alone receives hundreds of candidate names a day, but the vast majority lead nowhere; there's just one oddball for a hundred thousand candidates.

Given the circumstances, I considered it best to change the subject.

T. Glumov.

(END OF DOCUMENT 10)

DOCUMENT 11

WORKING RECORDING
Date: May 9, '99.
Participants: M. Kammerer, director of UE Department; T. Glumov, inspector
Subject: 009, "The Visit of the Old Lady"
Contents: The Oddball Institute as a possible object of interest for subject 009

KAMMERER: That is curious. You're quite the observer, boy. Your eye is the best spy! Of course you have a theory already. Go ahead.

GLUMOV: The conclusion or the thinking?

KAMMERER: The thinking, please.

GLUMOV: It would be simplest to assume that it was some metapsychology enthusiast who reported Albina and Kir to the Institute in Kharkov. If someone like that witnessed the events in Malaya Pesha, he or she could have been surprised by the anomalous reaction of those two, and therefore reported it to the relevant organization. In my estimation, there are three people who could have done that. Basil Neverov of the emergency crew. Oleg Pankratov, the lecturer and former astroarchaelogist. And his wife, Zosya Lyadova, the painter. Of course, they were not exactly witnesses in the literal sense, but that isn't relevant. I didn't risk talking to any of them without your permission, but I consider it quite possible to learn from them directly whether they passed information to the Institute or not.

KAMMERER: There's a simpler way—

GLUMOV: Yes, using the index. Ask the Institute directly. But this isn't an acceptable way forward at all, and here's why: If it's some well-meaning enthusiast, everything will be cleared up and the matter will be over. I'm suggesting we examine another possibility. Namely, that there were no well-meaning enthusiasts, but rather a special observer from the Oddball Institute was on site.

(Pause)

Let's suppose that a special observer from the Oddball Institute was in Malaya Pesha. That would mean that a psychological experiment took place with the goal of, let's say, identifying unusual people among regular ones. To, for example, later check these unusual people for being oddballs, as they call it. In this case, two possibilities exist. One is that the Oddball Institute is a regular research center, with regular researchers performing regular experiments—of a rather dubious ethical nature, but ultimately aiming to advance science. But then it's unclear how they could have access to technology that is well ahead of our most advanced embryomechanics and bioconstruction.

(Pause)

The other possibility is that the experiment in Malaya Pesha was not conducted by humans, as we had already assumed. What is the Oddball Institute in light of that?

(Pause)

Then the Institute is no institute at all, their oddballs are no oddballs, and the employees are most certainly not working on metapsychology.

KAMMERER: What then? What are they working on, and who are they?

GLUMOV: So you find my arguments to be unconvincing again?

KAMMERER: On the contrary, my boy. On the contrary! They're all too convincing, these arguments of yours. But I would like you to make your idea clear, direct, and unambiguous. Like in a report.

GLUMOV: Of course. The so-called Oddball Institute is in actuality a Wanderer tool to sort people according to some criteria currently unknown to me. That's it.

KAMMERER: Consequently, Daniel Logovenko, their deputy director, my old friend—

GLUMOV (interrupting): No! That would be too fantastic. But maybe your Daniel Logovenko was sorted a long time ago? His long-lasting friendship with you does not preclude that. He's been sorted and is working for the Wanderers. As the rest of the Institute's staff, not to mention their oddballs . . .

(Pause)

They have been conducting this sorting for at least twenty years. When enough people got sorted, they organized the Institute, put their oscillating frequency chambers up and put ten thousand people a year through them under the pretense of looking for oddballs . . . and we don't know how many other such organizations exist on the planet under different guises.

(Pause)

And Sorcerer ran out of the Institute and back to Saraksh not because he was offended or had an upset stomach. He sensed the Wanderers! Like our whales did, or the lemmings. "When the blind can see the seeing," that is about us. "And misses all that closer lies," that's also about us, Big Bug!

(Pause)

To put it briefly, we might be able to catch the Wanderers for the first time in history.

KAMMERER: Yes, and all of this because you noticed two names on a display . . . By the way, are you sure it really was a coincidence? (Hurriedly) OK, fine, let's not discuss that. What are you suggesting?

GLUMOV: Me?

KAMMERER: Yes. You.

GLUMOV: W-Well, if you want my opinion . . . our next steps are obvious, in my opinion. First of all we have to catch Wanderers there, and expose the sorted people. Set up covert mentoscopy, and if necessary, subject everyone there to the deepest mentoscopy by force. I presume they are prepared and would block their memory . . . No big deal, that would be evidence against them. If they can present fake memories, that would be worse . . .

KAMMERER: Fine, enough. You did a great job, I commend you. Now here's your assignment. Prepare lists of the following people for me. First, people with the inverse Penguin syndrome—everyone registered by the medics up to now. Second, people who did not undergo fukamization—

GLUMOV (interrupting): That's over one million people!

KAMMERER: No, I mean people who refused the maturity vaccine, that's twenty thousand people. Some work to do, but we have to be prepared. And third, take all of our data about mysterious disappearances and make a list.

GLUMOV: Including those who reappeared later?

KAMMERER: In particular them. Sandro is working on it; I'll tell him to work with you. That's it.

GLUMOV: An inverse syndrome list, a refuser list, a list of reappearances. Understood. And still, Big Bug . . .

KAMMERER: Say it.

GLUMOV: Would you allow me to talk to Neverov and that couple from Malaya Pesha?

KAMMERER: To clean your conscience?

GLUMOV: Yes. What if it was a simple well-meaning enthusiast . . .

KAMMERER: Permission granted. (Short pause) I wonder what you'd do if it does turn out to be an enthusiast . . .

(END OF DOCUMENT 11)

✦✦✦

I listened to the recording again now. My voice was young then, important, confident, the voice of a man who decides fates, for whom no mysteries exist in the past, present, or future, a man who knows what he's doing and that he is right. I'm amazed now at what a great actor and hypocrite I was then. In reality, I was just barely holding on. I already had an action plan ready, I was waiting for the president's authorization that never came, I was trying and failing to gather the courage to go to Komov without that authorization.

Despite all that, I clearly remember the joy I experienced that morning, listening to Toivo Glumov and watching him. It was his hour. He had been looking for them, the inhumans infiltrating his Earth, for five years, with constant setbacks, almost alone, rewarded with nothing and by nobody, tortured by the condescension of his beloved wife; he looked and he found them. Was right. Was more perceptive, patient, serious than them all—the jokers, the amateur philosophers, the intellectual ostriches.

I am of course ascribing this celebratory feeling to him. In the moment, I think he felt nothing other than a painful impatience to finally grab the enemy by the throat. Because, having clearly proven that the enemy was on Earth and acting, he still had no idea just what he had really proven.

But I did. And still, looking at him that morning, I was in awe of him, I was proud of him, I admired him; he could have been my son, and I wish I had a son like that.

I gave him a heap of work mainly because I wanted to have him in his office, behind a desk. There was no response from the Institute, and the work on the lists had to be done anyway.

DOCUMENT 12

COMCON-2, Ural-North
Date: May 10, '99
Author: Inspector T. Glumov
Subject: 009, "The Visit of the Old Lady"
Contents: The information on Malaya Pesha events was transmit-
ted to the Oddball Institute by O. O. Pankratov

According to your authorization, I conducted conversations with
B. Neverov, O. Pankratov, and Z. Lyadova with the aim of clarify-
ing whether one of them had transmitted to the Oddball Institute
information about the anomalous behavior of certain individuals
during the events in Malaya Pesha on the night of May 6.

1. The conversation with emergency crewman Basil Neverov
took place yesterday around noon, by videocall. The conversation
was of no operational interest. B. Neverov was definitely hearing
about the Oddball Institute for the first time.

2. I met Oleg Olegovich Pankratov and his wife Zosya Lyadova
unofficially at a regional conference of amateur astroarchaelo-
gists in Syktyvkar. During a light conversation over coffee, Oleg
Olegovich enthusiastically continued a conversation I had started
about the Oddball Institute's wonders, and by his own will, with
no further encouragement from me, conveyed the following facts:

- he has for many years now been an activist of the Oddball
  Institute and even has his own index as a constant source of
  information,
- it was his efforts that led metapsychologists to notice such
  amazing people as Rita Gluzskaya ("the Dark Eye"), Lebey

Malang (a psychoparamorph), and Konstantin Movzon ("the Fifth Lord of the Flies"),

- he is very grateful to me for the information about the wondrous Albina and the incredible Kir, which I so kindly and timely provided to him in Malaya Pesha, information that he immediately relayed to the Institute,
- he has visited the Institute personally three times, attending the yearly activist conference. He doesn't know Daniel Alexandrovich Logovenko personally but highly respects him as a distinguished scientist.

3. In light of the above, I consider my previous report 018/99 to be of no interest within the scope of subject 009.

T. Glumov.

(END OF DOCUMENT 12)

DOCUMENT 13

To: M. Kammerer, Director, UE
From: T. Glumov, Inspector

REQUEST
I hereby request a vacation leave for six months in order to accompany my wife on a lengthy work trip to Pandora.
T. Glumov, 05/10/99.

RESOLUTION. Denied. Continue work as assigned.
M. Kammerer. 05/10/99.

(END OF DOCUMENT 13)

UNCONVENTIONAL EVENTS DEPARTMENT, OFFICE D, MAY 11, '99

On the morning of May 11, a grim Toivo came to work and read my resolution. He must have calmed down during the night. He neither protested nor insisted, but went to his office D and started working on the list of inverse Penguin syndrome cases, of which he soon found seven, but only two had names; the rest were listed as "patient Z., servomechanic," "Theodore P., ethno-linguist," and the like.

Around noon, a scruffy, haggard, and sickly Sandro Mtbevari showed up in office D. Sitting down behind his desk, with no introductions or jokes like he used to make after longer trips, he reported to Toivo that he would now report to him, under Big Bug's orders, but would first like to finish his report on the trip. Toivo carefully asked what the problem was, taken aback by the state Sandro was in. An annoyed Sandro answered that the problem was that something had happened to him, and it wasn't clear if it should be in the report and, if so, how it should be presented.

He immediately began to recount, struggling to pick words, getting confused in the details, and nervously laughing at himself the whole time.

That morning, he walked out of the null-T booth in the resort town of Rosalinde (not far from Biarritz), walked three miles along a rocky, deserted path among the vineyards, and arrived at his destination around ten o'clock—the Rose Valley was below him. The path continued downward, toward the Winds of Fortune manor, its pointed roof visible through the thick greenery. Sandro noted the time out of habit: it was one minute to ten, as he had planned. Before starting his descent toward the manor, he sat down on a round black boulder and shook pebbles out of his sandals. It was very hot, the boulder was burning through his clothes, and he was very thirsty.

That must be when he got ill. His ears started ringing, and the sunny day seemed suddenly hazy. He imagined himself going down the path, walking without feeling his legs, past a funny gazebo he hadn't seen from above, past an open glider with the engine taken apart, past a huge furry dog that lay in the shadow and looked at him indifferently, panting with its tongue out. Then he took the steps up to a veranda overgrown with roses. He could hear the steps creaking but still didn't feel his own legs. In the depth of the veranda, there was a table covered by strange items, and there, arms spread wide, the man he needed was leaning above the table.

The man lifted his small eyes, seated deep under his gray eyebrows, and his face turned to light disappointment. Sandro introduced himself and, not hearing his own voice, started to present his cover story, but he hadn't said more than a few sentences when the man frowned, said something along the lines of "Well, isn't this bad timing?" and then Sandro came to, drenched in sweat and holding his right sandal. He was sitting on the boulder, the hot granite burning through his shorts, and his watch still showed one minute to ten. Maybe ten or fifteen seconds had passed, not more.

He put his sandals on, wiped his face, and that must be when he got bad again. He was again going down the path, not feeling his legs, watching the world as if through a neutral color filter, and he had *Well, I have some bad timing* repeating in his head. Again the funny gazebo on the left (a legless doll with one arm was on its floor), again the glider (a gutsy little devil painted on its side), and another glider was there, farther in, its bonnet also open, and the dog was now napping, its heavy head resting on its paws. (A strange dog . . . was it a dog?) Creaking steps. The cool veranda. The man again, peering out from below his gray eyebrows, frowning and speaking in a pretend threatening voice, like to an unruly child, "What did I tell you? This isn't the time!

Shoo!" And Sandro came to again, not sitting on the boulder anymore but on the sharp grass next to it, and he was nauseated.

What is it with me today? he thought with fear and disappointment as he tried to compose himself. The world still looked muted, his ears were ringing, but Sandro was in control now. It was almost exactly ten, he was very thirsty but no longer weak, and he had to finish what he came for. He rose and then he saw that same man step out of the vegetation and onto the path, and stop right there, looking toward Sandro, and then that furry dog also followed and stood by the man, watching Sandro, who then noted that it was no dog but a young bighead. Sandro lifted a hand, without knowing whether in greeting or to call attention to himself, and the world got black, tumbling out of Sandro's view.

When he regained his senses again, he found himself sitting on a bench in the resort of Rosalinde, next to the null-T booth he had arrived by. He still felt nauseous and thirsty, but the world was clear and welcoming; the time was forty-two past ten. Carefree, well-dressed people walked by, looking at him in concern as they slowed down, and then a cyberwaiter rolled up with a tall, sweaty glass of some local specialty . . .

After listening to the entire story, Toivo sat in silence for some time, and then said, choosing his words slowly, "This definitely has to be included in the report."

"Let's assume so," Sandro said. "But how to present it?"

"Write it as you just told me."

"I told you as if I got woozy from the heat and I saw all that in delirium."

"So you are not sure that you were delirious?"

"How should I know? I could tell the same story as if I got hypnotized, or if it was an induced hallucination . . ."

"Do you think the bighead caused the hallucination?"

"I don't know. Could be. But probably not. He was too far from me, seventy-five yards, no less than that . . . and he was too young for such tricks. Also, why would he?"

After some silence, Toivo asked, "What did Big Bug say?"

"Uh, I couldn't utter a word. He didn't even glance at me. 'I'm busy, you report to Glumov.'"

"Tell me then," Toivo spoke, "are you sure you never really went down to the house?"

"I am not sure about anything. I'm only sure something is very much not right with these Van Winkles. I've been dealing with them since the beginning of the year, but there's no clarity. Worse, it gets more confusing with every case. But not like today, this was something extra . . ."

Toivo uttered through his teeth, "You do understand what this looks like if it really happened, right?" He remembered: "Wait, the registrator! What's on your registrator?"

Sandro answered with a look of complete resignation to his fate: "There is nothing on my registrator. It was off."

"Oh, come on!"

"I know—but I definitely remember recharging and turning it on before going."

DOCUMENT 14

COMCON-2, Ural-North
Report 047/99
Date: May 4–11, '99
Author: Inspector S. Mtbevari
Subject: 101, "Rip Van Winkle"
Contents: Inspection results of the "'80s group"

Received your orders to inspect on the morning of May 4. Immediately commenced to proceed.

MAY 4, BY 10:40 PM
Yuri Nikolayevich Astangov. Not present at the recorded address. No new address in the GWI. A survey of relatives, friends, and coworkers produced no results. The general response was, we can't say anything, we haven't been in touch for years, after his return in '95 he became even more of a loner than before the disappearance. A check of the cosmodrome network, the near-Earth null-T system, and production cooperatives (with elevated degree of danger) produced no result. Supposition: Just like last time, he "retreated to solitude deep in the Amazon to perfect his new philosophy." (It would be interesting to speak to someone familiar with his previous philosophies. The doctors say otherwise, but I think he's just nuts.)

MAY 6, BY 11:30 PM
Fernan Leer. Met me at the recorded address at 11:05 AM. I presented my cover story; we conversed until 12:50. F. Leer claimed to be feeling very well, not experiencing any unpleasant symptoms, not having any consequences from the amnesia of '89–'91, and therefore seeing no need to undergo a mentoscopy. He has

nothing to add to his statements from '91, because he still does not remember anything. He has long since lost interest in trans-mantle engineering and has devoted the last several years to the design and study of multidimensional games. During our conversation, he was cordial but absentminded. He got more animated when the idea of teaching me to play snip-snap-snurr occurred to him. That concluded our meeting. (Verified: F. Leer has indeed become an expert on multidimensional games; he is known as the "entertainer for academics.")

Albert Oskarovich Tuul. Not present at the recorded address. New address in the GWI: Venusborg (Venus). Not present at that address either. According to the Venus Registration Office, A. Tuul has never been to Venus. In '97, he told his mother that he intended to work with the pathfinders at the Khius camp (on the planet Kala-i Mug). She regularly receives communications from him (most recently in March). These communications are long-winded letters that offer a detailed and rather literary description of attempts to find traces of the so-called werewolf civilization. According to Khius camp, A. Tuul has never been there but has regular null-comms calls with E. Kapustin, the excavator of the group, who is convinced that his good friend A. Tuul is living on Earth, at the control address. Kapustin most recently spoke to Tuul on January 1. A check of the cosmodrome network indicates multiple trips to Deep Space since '96 (the year of reappearance), the last return trip from Resort in October '98. A check of near-Earth null-T indicates multiple visits to the Moon, Orangery, and BOP. A check of production cooperative systems indicates employment as a chef from December '96 to October '97 at the abyssal laboratory Tuscarora-16. Supposition: A. Tuul is a highly careless man with a low feeling of social responsibility, the incident of '89 taught him nothing, and he still pays no attention to insignificant details such as having the correct address on record.

MAY 8, BY 10:10 PM

Maurice Amazaspovich Bagrationi. Not present at the recorded address. No new address in the GWI. Has no close relatives that he has regular contact with due to his advanced age. Work-related communications ceased twenty-five years ago. Neither of his old friends, known to us from the investigation into his disappearance in '81, are present at their control addresses, their whereabouts cannot be ascertained. Check of the cosmodrome, near-Earth null-T, production cooperatives: nothing. Information from the Gerontology Center: unable to contact him for an examination for many years. Supposition: An unregistered accident. Locating his friends to inform them seems appropriate.

Martin Zhang. Not present at the recorded address. New address in the GWI: Matrix Base (Secunda, EN 7113). Sent to Matrix Base as an interpreter in January '93 by the Bioconfiguration Institute (London). Currently (since December '99) on an extended vacation, whereabouts unknown. Check of the cosmodrome network, near-Earth null-T, and production cooperatives since December '98: nothing. A curiosity: S. Wang, a neighbor at M. Zhang's control address, reports seeing M. Zhang in March of this year. He saw M. Zhang land a glider in his garden and, without entering the house, begin taking the glider apart. He returned S. Wang's greeting carelessly and avoided a conversation. S. Wang left on his errands and returned a few hours later, at which point M. Zhang and the glider were gone and did not reappear. This seems interesting because in M. Zhang's first disappearance, neither his departure nor his arrival were noted by registrators of the cosmodrome network. Question: Do living organisms exist whose genetic code is not detected or properly identified by the existing registration systems? Supposition: Considering that M. Zhang is known to the Krakow Regeneration Institute due to his regeneration of both legs, and since he has never returned to Krakow for screening after his regeneration, the Matrix Base should be informed that continued avoidance of a screening might have severe consequences for M. Zhang. I have such a warning notice; the institute is quite concerned about M. Zhang's irresponsible behavior.

MAY 9, BY 9:30 PM

Cyprian Okigbo. Received me at the recorded address at 10:15 AM. He was polite and pleasant but seemed to be thinking about something else. He seated me in the living room, offered a glass of coconut milk, listened to my cover story, and with the words "By God, this is not funny!" disappeared somewhere in the house with a concerned look. I waited for him for an hour, then searched the house. Did not find anyone. The study, both bedrooms, and the attic had all their windows open but no prints under any of them. In the workshop (?) the windows were tightly closed and covered with metallic blinds; it was intolerably cold (possibly low twenties; the water in the aquarium was covered with a thin layer of ice). No sign of any refrigeration device. The robe C. Okigbo was wearing when he met me was on the floor of the study. I waited for two more hours, then spoke to the neighbors. Nothing substantial: C. Okigbo is a private man, receives no guests, spends most of his time at home, does not care for his garden, but is nonetheless kind, likes children and infants in particular, is good with them. Supposition: Could I have hallucinated being received by C. Okigbo? (See report 048/99.)

MAY 11, BY 10:45 AM

While attempting to establish whether Émile Fare Alais is at the recorded address, I experienced an episode of nausea and delirium. Being unable to determine whether that is a personal matter or of interest to the case, I present a separate report 048/99 on the episode.

Sandro Mtbevari

(END OF DOCUMENT 14)

✦✦✦

I never found out what Toivo Glumov thought about Sandro Mtbevari's inspections. I think he was amazed, not so much by the results as by the idea that he had underestimated the opponent's truly incredible power.

I did not see Toivo on the eleventh, nor the twelfth or thirteenth. Those were probably his most difficult days, when he was adapting to his new role, that of young knight Alyosha Popovich who expected to merely face the grotesque Idolische, only to see the malicious god Loki in front of him. But on each of those days I remembered Toivo and thought about him, because for me the morning of May 11 began with two documents.

DOCUMENT 15

To: Director, UE Department
From: The President

Dear Big Bug!
I cannot help it, they're going to take me in for a surgery. It's not all bad news, though. G. Komov will assume my duties (starting tomorrow, I think), in addition to his own. I passed all of my materials on to him. I won't lie, he was skeptical of them. But he knows me, and he knows you. He is prepared now, so you have the chance to convince him, especially if you were able to get new evidence as you planned. And then you will be dealing with not just the president of a COMCON-2 sector but with an influential World Council member. I wish you luck—wish me the same.
Athos
05/11/99

(END OF DOCUMENT 15)

DOCUMENT 16

Mak!

1. Toivo Alexandrovich Glumov taken under observation today (registered on 05/08).

2. Also taken under observation today:

- Artek Kaskazi, 18, student, Tehran. 05/07.
- Charles Mauki, 63, marine technician, Odessa. 05/08.

Lab Tech
May 11, '99

[END OF DOCUMENT 16]

✦✦✦

It is probably strange, but I have almost no memory of my thoughts regarding Lab Tech's incredible message. I only remember the feeling of a sudden, sneaky slap in the face—out of nowhere and for no reason, from behind a corner, when you're expecting something else entirely. Resentment, like a child's, to the point of tears, that is what I remember, that is that remains of the probably whole hour I spent staring unseeingly with my jaw hanging open.

I must have had some pointless thoughts about backstabbing, about treason. I must have felt fury, irritation, and deep disappointment from having a plan of action, in which everyone had their role to play and now the plan had a gaping hole on it that could not be mended. And there was sorrow, of course, the desperate sorrow of losing a friend, a companion, a son.

More precisely, it was a temporary madness, a chaos not even of feelings but of their shreds.

Then I slowly came to and started thinking—coldly and methodically, as I had to think in my situation.

The wind from the gods births storms, but it also fills the sails.

Thinking coldly and methodically on that cloudy morning, I did after all find a new role for the new Toivo Glumov in my plan. And this new role seemed not less but much more important than the old. My plan had become a long-term one, and we were going to attack, not defend.

I contacted Komov the same day and he scheduled a meeting for the following day, May 12.

Early on the morning of the twelfth, he saw me in the president's office. I presented all my materials to him. Our conversation took five hours. My plan was approved with only minor adjustments. (I do not dare claim that I managed to dispel Komov's skepticism entirely, but there was no doubt that he was curious.)

Also on the twelfth, I returned to my office and, in the tradition of Hontian infiltrators, spent a few minutes with my fingers pressed to my temples, thinking about the sublime, and then I called Grisha Serosovin in and gave him a task. At 6:05 PM, he reported its completion. All I had to do was wait.

On the morning of the thirteenth, Daniel Logovenko called.

DOCUMENT 17

WORKING RECORDING
Date: May 13, '99
Participants: M. Kammerer, director of UE Department; D. Logovenko, deputy director of the Kharkov branch of the IMS
Subject: ✱✱✱
Contents: ✱✱✱

LOGOVENKO: Hello, Maxim, it's me.
KAMMERER: Greetings. What do you have to say?
LOGOVENKO: I have to say it was impressive work.
KAMMERER: Glad you liked it.
LOGOVENKO: I cannot say I liked it, but I have to give credit to an old friend.
(Pause)
    I take it to mean that you want to meet me and have an honest talk.
KAMMERER: Yes. But not me. And maybe not you.
LOGOVENKO: It will have to be me. But if not you, who then?
KAMMERER: Komov.
LOGOVENKO: Oh! So you after all decided to—
KAMMERER: Komov is currently my direct superior.
LOGOVENKO: Ah, I see . . . fine. Where and when?
KAMMERER: Komov wants Gorbovsky to participate in the conversation.
LOGOVENKO: Leonid Andreievich? But he's dying . . .
KAMMERER: Exactly. Let him hear all of this. From you.
(Pause)
LOGOVENKO: Yes. Seems it really is time to have a talk.
KAMMERER: Tomorrow, at three o'clock sharp, at Gorbovsky's. You know his home? Near Krāslava, on the banks of the Daugava.

LOGOVENKO: Yes, I know. Until tomorrow. Was that all?

KAMMERER: That's all. Until tomorrow.

(The conversation took place between 09:02 and 09:04 AM.)

[END OF DOCUMENT 17]

✦ ✦ ✦

It's remarkable that the Ludens Group, despite all of their insistence and tenacity, never bothered me about Daniel Alexandrovich Logovenko. I and Daniel had known one another since long-forgotten times, the blessed '60s, when I, a young and exceedingly energetic COMCONite, was taking a special course in psychology at Kiev University, where Daniel, a young and exceedingly energetic metapsychologist, taught my hands-on lessons, and in the evenings we would pursue with great vigor the charming and exceedingly capricious young women of Kiev. He definitely saw something in me among all the students; we became friends and met regularly in the early years. Then our studies separated us; we got together less frequently and hadn't seen each other from the early '80s until the recent tea at my house just before these events. He turned out to be very unhappy in his family life, and now I understand why. He was very unhappy in general, and that is not something I can say about myself.

Anyone who seriously studies the time of the Great Revelation tends to feel confident in their knowledge of who Daniel Logovenko is. What a mistake! What does a person who read Newton's complete works know about the man himself? Yes, Logovenko played an extremely important role in the Great Revelation. The Logovenko impulse, Logovenko's T wave, the Logovenko declaration, the Logovenko committee . . .

But do you know what happened to Logovenko's wife?

Or how he ended up at a special course in advanced and anomalous ethology in the city of Split?

Or why, among all the students back in '66, he especially noted M. Kammerer, a promising energetic COMCONite?

Or what D. Logovenko thought about the Great Revelation—not what he declared, or proclaimed, or preached, but what he thought and felt deep down in his inhuman heart?

There are many questions like that. Some of them I could, I think, answer fully. Others I could only guess. And the rest have no answers, and never will.

DOCUMENT 18

COMCON-2. Ural-North.
Report 020/99
Date: May 13, '99
Author: Inspector T. Glumov.
Subject: 009, "The Visit of the Old Lady"
Contents: Cross-referencing the list of inverse Penguin syndrome
sufferers with the "Subject" list

As you instructed, I compiled a list of inverse Penguin syndrome
cases using all available sources. In total I found 12 cases, of which
10 could be identified. Comparing the list of identified inverse
cases with the "S" list, the following persons appear on both:

1. Ivan Georgievich Krivoklykov, 65, psychiatrist, Lemboi base
   (EN 2105).
2. Alf Christian Pakkala, 31, construction operator, Alaskan
   Construction Organization, Anchorage.
3. Nika Jo, 48, a designer/weaver, Irrawaddy Factory, Pyapon.
4. Albert Oskarovich Tuul, 59, chef, whereabouts unknown
   (refer to report 047/99 by S. Mtbevari).

The degree of overlap seems to be strikingly high to me.
Even more striking is the fact that A. O. Tuul essentially appears
on three lists.

I consider it necessary to refer to you the full list of people
with inverse Penguin syndrome. The list is attached.

T. Glumov

(END OF DOCUMENT 18)

LEONID'S HOUSE (KRĀSLAVA, LATVIA), MAY 14, '99, 3:00 PM

Daugava was quick, narrow, and clear as it flowed past Krāslava. The dry sand of the beach was a yellow line from which a steep, sandy slope ran to the pine trees. An oval landing pad with a white-and-gray checkered pattern floated above the water, carelessly parked fliers baking in the sun. Three of them in total—old-fashioned, heavy vehicles only used by old people born in the previous century.

Toivo reached for the glider's door, but I stopped him. "Don't. Wait."

I was looking up, where the cream-colored walls of a house peeked out from behind the pines, where ancient stairs, their wood gray with age, zigzagged down the slope. Someone in white was slowly descending down those stairs, a heavyset, almost cube-shaped, visibly old man, his right arm on the handrail, one step at a time, deliberately setting his feet, the sun reflecting off his big bald head. I recognized the man. It was August Johann Bader, a cosmotrooper and a pathfinder. A ruin of a heroic age.

"Let's wait for him to come down," I said. "I don't want to meet him."

I turned and started looking in the other direction, at the other coast of the river, and Toivo also turned tactfully, and so we sat until we heard the creaking of the stairs and the wheezing, heavy breathing accompanied by some other inappropriate sounds that could be sobbing, and so the old man went past our glider, dragged his feet on the plastic, and appeared in my field of view, and I involuntarily looked into his face.

This close the face seemed unrecognizable. It was contorted with grief. His soft cheeks were hanging down, his mouth was open in resignation, tears streamed from swollen eyes.

Hunching, Bader approached an ancient green-and-yellow flier, the most ancient of the three, with some stupid bumps on the rear, with ugly vision slits for its antique autopilot, dented sides, and dull nickel handles—he approached, opened the door, and then, croaking or sobbing, climbed into the cabin.

Nothing happened for a long time. The flier was standing, door open, and the old man inside was either trying to compose himself before flying off, or was crying, his bald head on the decrepit oval controls. Then, finally, a brown hand stretched out of his white sleeve and closed the door. The ancient vehicle rose soundlessly and with unexpected lightness, and rose above the river's steep banks.

"That was Bader," I said. "He said his good-byes. Let's go."

We got out of the glider and started up the stairs. I said, without turning toward Toivo, "No emotions. You're coming here to report. It will be a very important work conversation. Don't relax."

"A work conversation sounds great," Toivo replied to my back. "But it seems to me now isn't the time for work conversations."

"You're wrong. Now is the time. As for Bader . . . don't think about that now. Think about the matter at hand."

"Very well," Toivo said obediently.

Gorbovsky's home, "Leonid's House," was completely standard, the typical architecture of the start of the century: favored by space explorers, deep ocean divers, and transmantle workers who missed rural life—no workshop, no stables, no kitchen . . . but with a small power station to serve the personal null-device that Gorbovsky, as a member of the World Council, was entitled to. And all around there were pines, thick heather shrubs, it smelled of warm fir needles, and bees buzzed sleepily in the still air.

We climbed to the veranda and entered the house through wide-open doors. In the living room, curtains drawn and only a small lamp by the couch lit, sat a man, his legs crossed, studying a map or a mentoscheme by the lamp. It was Komov.

"Good day," I said, and Toivo bowed silently.

"Good day, good day," Komov said, seemingly impatient. "Come in, sit down. He's sleeping. That damn Bader wore him out completely . . . Are you Glumov?"

"Yes," Toivo said.

Komov studied him closely and with interest. I gave a small cough, and Komov asked, "Is your mother Maya Toivovna Glumova, by any chance?"

"Yes," Toivo said.

"I've had the honor of working with her," Komov said.

"Yes?" Toivo said.

"Yes. Hasn't she told you? Operation Ark . . ."

"Yes, I know that story," Toivo said.

"What is Maya Toivovna working on now?"

"Xenotechnology."

"Where? Under whom?"

"The Sorbonne. Under Saligny, I think."

Komov nodded. He was still staring at Toivo. His eyes were gleaming. As if seeing Maya Glumova's adult son made him relive some intense memories.

I coughed again, and Komov turned to look at me. "By the way, if you want some refreshments, there are drinks here, in the bar. We will have to wait. I don't want to wake him. He's smiling in his sleep. Dreaming of something good . . . Bader and his sniveling be damned!"

"What do the doctors say?" I asked.

"The same. 'No will to live.' There is no medicine against that . . . or there is, but he doesn't want to take it. He got tired of living, that's the problem. We cannot understand it . . . the man is over a hundred and fifty. Tell me please, Glumov, what does your father do?"

"I don't see him much," Toivo said. "I think he is now a hybridizer. On Yaila, I think."

"And you—" Komov began, but fell silent as a weak raspy voice came from the depths of the house: "Gennady! Who's there with you? Let them come."

"Let's go." Komov jumped to his feet.

The bedroom windows were wide open. Gorbovsky lay on the couch, a checkered blanket up to his head, and he looked incredibly tall, thin, and gut-wrenchingly miserable. His cheeks were sullen, the famous shoe-shaped nose stiff, his sunken eyes sorrowful and bleak. They no longer wanted to see, but they had to and did.

"Ahh, Max, dear," Gorbovsky uttered when he saw me. "You're as handsome as ever . . . I'm happy to see you, I am."

That was a lie. He wasn't happy to see dear Max. He wasn't happy about anything. He must have thought that he offered a friendly smile, but in reality his face was a grimace of dreary politeness. Endless and condescending patience emanated from him. As if Leonid Andreievich was thinking, so someone's come again, this cannot take too long, they will leave as all before them did, and leave me in peace . . .

"And who is this?" asked Gorbovsky, with a visible effort to suppress his apathy.

"This is Toivo Glumov," Komov said. "A COMCONite, inspector. I've told you—"

"Yes, yes," said Gorbovsky weakly. "You have. I remember. 'The Visit of the Old Lady' . . . Sit down, Toivo, my boy. I am listening."

Toivo sat and looked at me quizzically.

"Expound on your point of view," I said. "And justify it."

Toivo began: "I will now formulate a certain theorem. The formulation is not mine. Dr. Bromberg formulated it five years ago. The theorem, then. In the early eighties, a certain super-civilization that we will refer to as the Wanderers for brevity commenced active progressor activity on our planet. One of the goals of this activity is selection. By various means, the Wanderers are selecting out of all humanity certain individuals who are, by criteria known to the Wanderers, suitable for . . . for example, suitable for contact. Or for subsequent advancement as a species. Or even for transformation into Wanderers. The Wanderers likely have other goals that we do not suspect, but it is now perfectly clear to me that they are performing selection and sorting here, and I will try to prove that now."

Toivo fell silent. Komov was looking at him intently. Gorbovsky might have been sleeping if it weren't for his fingers, joined on his chest, sometimes coming into motion, drawing intricate patterns in the air. Then he, without opening his eyes, spoke: "Gennady, bring our guests something to drink . . . they must be hot . . ."

I jumped to my feet, but Komov stopped me. "I'll bring it," he muttered, and left the room.

"Continue, my boy," Gorbovsky asked.

Toivo went ahead and continued. He explained Penguin syndrome: using some kind of grid the Wanderers erected in sector 41/02, they were apparently disqualifying people with a hidden cosmophobia and selecting hidden cosmophiles. He explained the Malaya Pesha events, how, using clearly alien biotechnology, the Wanderers conducted an experiment to disqualify xenophobes and identify xenophiles. He explained the push for the Amendment. Fukamization was seemingly either a hurdle to the sorting operation or could have eliminated some qualities the Wanderers needed in future generations of humanity, so they somehow organized and successfully conducted a campaign to make the procedure optional. Year by year, the number of selectees, for lack of a better word, kept growing; it could not remain unnoticed, we had to take note of these selectees, and we did. The disappearances in the '80s, the sudden transformations of ordinary people into geniuses, Sandro Mtbevari's recent discovery of people with fantastic powers . . . and, finally, the so-called Oddball Institute in Kharkov is doubtlessly a Wanderer sorting center.

"They are not even really hiding," Toivo clarified. "They apparently feel powerful enough to no longer fear discovery. It is possible that they believe we can no longer change anything. I'm not sure . . . Well, I'm done. I would only like to add that, of course, we have only uncovered a small fraction of their whole range of activities. That has to be kept in mind. And in conclusion, I consider it necessary to say a few good words about Dr. Bromberg, who had essentially no definitive information but was already able five years ago to deduce literally all of the phenomena we've seen: mass phobias, sudden appearance of talents in people, and even irregularities in the behavior of animals, such as whales."

Toivo turned to me. "I'm done," he said.

I nodded. Nobody said a word.

"Wanderers, Wanderers," Gorbovsky almost sang. He had pulled up his blanket all the way up to his nose. "For as long as I remember, from my childhood, so much talk of these Wanderers . . . You really dislike them for some reason, Toivo, my boy. Why?"

"I dislike progressors," Toivo responded reservedly, and immediately added, "Leonid Andreievich, I used to be a progressor myself—"

"Nobody likes progressors," Gorbovsky mumbled. "Not even the progressors themselves." He let out a deep sigh and closed his eyes again. "To be honest, I don't see a problem here. These are all witty interpretations, no more than that. Give your materials to teachers, for instance, and they will have their own, no less witty. Deep ocean divers would have their own . . . They all have their own myths, their own Wanderers . . . Do not be offended, Toivo, but the very mention of Bromberg made me suspicious—"

"Speaking of which, all of Bromberg's work on the Monocosm has disappeared," Komov remarked quietly.

"But of course, he never had any works!" Gorbovsky laughed weakly. "You didn't know Bromberg. He was a noxious old man with an unimaginable imagination. Max sent him his anxious query. Bromberg, who had never devoted a single thought to these matters, sat in his cozy chair, stared into the air, and pulled the Monocosm hypothesis out of it there and then. It took him one evening. And he had forgotten all about it by the next day. He not only had a great imagination but was also an expert on forbidden science; his head was home to a ridiculous number of ridiculous analogies . . ."

As soon as Gorbovsky finished, Komov said, "Did I understand you, Glumov, correctly, that you claim there are Wanderers on Earth now? As creatures, I mean. As individuals."

"No," Toivo said. "I am not claiming that."

"Did I understand you, Glumov, correctly, that you claim there are accomplices of the Wanderers living and acting on Earth? Selectees, as you called them."

"Yes."

"Can you name any?"

"Yes. With a certain probability."

"Name them."

"Albert Oskarovich Tuul. Almost definitely. Cyprian Okigbo. Martin Zhang. Émile Fare Alais. Also almost definitely. I have about a dozen more, but with less certainty."

"Have you spoken to any selectees?"

"I think I have. At the Oddball Institute. I think there are many of them there. But I cannot yet say for sure who they are."

"So you are saying that you do not know how to distinguish them?"

"Of course. They look just like us. But they can be identified. At least to a sufficiently high degree of probability. But I'm sure the Oddball Institute has some device that lets them identify their own unmistakably, for certain."

Komov shot me a quick glance. Toivo noticed it and said with a challenge in his voice, "Yes! I think this is not the time to be tactful! We'll have to overlook some higher humanist ideals! We're dealing with progressors, and we have to respond in kind!"

"Specifically?" Komov asked, leaning forward.

"The whole range of our operating methods! From infiltration to forced mentoscopy, from—"

And then Gorbovsky let out a long wail, and we all turned to him in fear. Komov even jumped to his feet. Leonid Andreievich was still fine, however. He lay just as before, only the fake politeness on his thin face had given way to a grimace of annoyed revulsion.

"What have you started here around me?" His voice was whiny. "You're adults here, not schoolchildren or students . . . Have you really no shame? This is why I dislike all this talk of Wanderers, and always have! It inevitably turns into this kind of panicky mystery claptrap! When will you all finally understand, it's mutually exclusive . . . If the Wanderers are a supercivilization, then they have no interest in us, they are beings with a different history, different interests, they don't have progressors, and out of the whole universe only we, humanity, have progressors, because such is our history, because we always cry over our own past . . . we cannot change it and so we try to at least help others, having failed to help ourselves at the right time . . . that is where progressors come from! And the Wanderers, even if their past is like ours, they are so removed from it that they cannot even remember it any more than we remember the struggling hominid who first tried to fashion a boulder into an axe." He paused. "Progressor work is as laughable for a supercivilization as it would be for us to found seminaries to train village cantors . . ."

He fell silent again, and just looked from one face to another for a very long time. I glanced at Toivo. Toivo averted his gaze and shrugged his right shoulder, as if indicating that he has some counterarguments but doesn't consider it appropriate to present them now. Komov was looking off to the side, his thick black eyebrows drawn together.

"Heh-heh," Gorbovsky croaked. "I haven't managed to persuade you. All right, I will try insults now. If a boy as green as our dear Toivo managed to, uh, catch these progressors with their pants down, then how the hell can they be Wanderers? Just think for a moment! Would a supercivilization really be incapable of doing their work without you bunch noticing? And if you did notice, then what damn kind of supercivilization is it? The whales went insane, so of course the Wanderers must be to blame! Get out of my sight, let me die in peace!"

We all rose. Komov reminded me in a low tone to wait in the living room.

I nodded.

Toivo confusedly bowed to Gorbovsky. The old man paid no attention. He was angrily staring at the ceiling, moving his pallid lips.

I left the room with Toivo. I closed the door behind me and heard the soft hiss of the activating soundproofing system.

Toivo immediately took up place on the living room couch by the lamp, put his hands on his knees, and froze. He didn't look at me. I was not on his mind.

In the morning, I had told him:

"*You're coming with me. You'll speak to Komov and Gorbovsky.*"

"*What for?*" *he asked in astonishment.*

"*What, did you think we'd manage without the World Council?*"

"*But why me?*"

"*Because I already did. Now it's your turn.*"

"*All right,*" *he said, pursing his lips.*

Toivo Glumov, he was a fighter. He never retreated. He could only be thrown back.

And so he had been thrown back. I watched him from a corner.

He sat motionless for some time, then absentmindedly flipped through the mentograms with colorful notes by doctors that were laid out on the low table. Then he stood up and paced between the dark room's corners, hands behind his back.

The house was shrouded in an impenetrable silence. No voices could be heard from the bedroom, no forest sounds behind the thick closed curtains. He didn't even hear his own footsteps.

His eyes got used to the darkness. Leonid Andreievich's living room was spartan. The lamp with an obviously homemade lampshade, a big couch next to it, and a low table. In the far corner, a few seats of clearly non-Earth manufacture intended for clearly non-Earth rears. In the other corner, some kind of exotic plant, or maybe an ancient hat rack. That was all the furniture. Although there was the bar cabinet, its door slightly open, revealing a complete selection for any taste. Above the bar, pictures hung in transparent frames, the largest the size of an album sheet.

Toivo walked up to the pictures and looked at them. These were children's drawings. Watercolor. Gouache. Stylus. Little houses next to big girls rising far above pine trees. Dogs (or bigheads?). An elephant. A tahorg. Some kind of space construct—could be a fantastic spaceship or a hangar . . . Toivo sighed and went back to the couch. I watched him intently.

He had tears in his eyes. He was no longer thinking about the lost battle. There, on the other side of that door, Gorbovsky was dying—an era was dying, a living legend was dying. Space explorer. Cosmotrooper. Discoverer of civilizations. Creator of the first COMCON. Member of the World Council. Grandpa Gorbovsky. Above all, Grandpa Gorbovsky. Indeed, Grandpa Gorbovsky. He was as if from a fairy tale, always kind and therefore always right. Such was his era that kindness always won. "Of all the possible solutions, choose the kindest." Not the most promising, not the most rational, not the most progressive, and certainly not the most effective—but the kindest! He had never said those words, and spared no sarcasm toward biographers who attributed those words to him, and he surely never thought those words, but his entire life's essence was in those words. And of course the words are no recipe; not everyone could be kind, it is a talent like an ear for music or clairvoyance, only even less common. And tears were welling up because the kindest of all people was dying. And his gravestone would say, HERE LIES THE KINDEST OF ALL.

I imagine Toivo was thinking all that. All of my hopes rested on the assumption that Toivo was thinking that.

Forty-three minutes passed.

The door was suddenly flung open. It was like a scene out of a fairy tale. Or a movie. Gorbovsky, incredibly tall in his striped pajamas, thin, jolly, took a few uncertain steps into the living room, dragging the checkered blanket behind him as its fringe caught on some button.

"Aha, you're still here!" he said with joyful satisfaction, speaking to the flabbergasted Toivo. "It's all ahead, my boy! It's all ahead! You're right!"

With those mysterious words, he rushed, staggering lightly, to the closest window and lifted the curtains. The room got blindingly light, we squinted, and Gorbovsky turned and stared at Toivo, who was standing at attention by the lamp. I looked at Komov. He was positively beaming, his sugar-white teeth flashing, looking happy like a cat that just ate a goldfish. He looked like an easygoing guy who had just told a brilliant joke. That was quite true, actually.

"Not bad, not bad!" Gorbovsky repeated. "Even excellent!"

He tilted his head, moved toward Toivo, very openly looking him up and down, got next to him, put a hand on his shoulder, and gave a light squeeze with his bony fingers.

"Well, I hope you will forgive my abrupt tone, my boy," Gorbovsky said, "but I was also right . . . And the abruptness is out of irritability. Dying is, I'll tell you, the nastiest of jobs. Pay no attention."

Toivo was silent. He, of course, understood nothing. Komov had thought this up and done it. Gorbovsky knew exactly as much as Komov saw fit to tell him. I could very well imagine the conversation they had just had in the bedroom. But Toivo Glumov understood nothing at all.

I took his elbow and said to Gorbovsky, "Leonid Andreievich, we are leaving."

Gorbovsky nodded a few times. "Go, of course. Thank you. You were of great help to me. We'll see each other again, many times."

When we were out on the porch, Toivo said, "Would you maybe explain what all that was?"

"You saw it: he changed his mind about dying," I said.

"Why?"

"It's a stupid question, Toivo, forgive me please . . ."

Toivo thought a bit and said, "And I am a fool. I've never felt so foolish in my entire life. Thank you for your thoughtfulness, Big Bug."

I only chuckled. We went down the steps toward the landing pad in silence. Some other man was walking up leisurely.

"All right," Toivo said, "should I continue working on the subject?"

"Of course."

"But I got ridiculed!"

"On the contrary. You made a great impression."

Toivo mumbled something under his breath. At the first landing we found ourselves face to face with the man who was walking upstairs. It was deputy director of the Kharkov IMS Daniel Alexandrovich Logovenko, looking flushed and very concerned.

"Greetings to you," he said to me. "I'm not too late, am I?"

"Not very," I replied. "He's waiting for you."

And then D. A. Logovenko gave the most conspiratorial of all winks to Toivo Glumov and continued up the steps, now visibly in a hurry. Toivo watched him go with a malicious squint.

DOCUMENT 19

Confidential!
Only for Presidium members of the World Council!
Copy 115

Contents: Recording of a conversation that took place at Leonid's House (Krāslava, Latvia) on May 14, '99
Participants: L. A. Gorbovsky, World Council member; G. Yu. Komov, World Council member, acting president of Ural-North COMCON-2 sector; D. A. Logovenko, deputy director of Kharkov IMS

KOMOV: So you are actually no different from a regular person?

LOGOVENKO: The difference is huge, but . . . now, when I am sitting here talking to you, I am only different in my knowledge that I am not like you. This is one of my levels . . . a rather tiring one, by the way. It does take me some effort, but I'm used to it, while most of us have lost touch with this level forever. And on this level, the differences can only be seen with special equipment.

KOMOV: You're saying that on different levels . . .

LOGOVENKO: Yes. On different levels, everything is different. A different consciousness, a different physiology . . . a different form, even.

KOMOV: So on other levels you are no longer human?

LOGOVENKO: We are not human at all. Do not be confused by the fact that we were birthed by humans and from humans . . .

GORBOVSKY: Excuse me, Daniel Alexandrovich. Could you perhaps demonstrate something . . . please do not misunderstand me, I do not wish to offend you, but so far . . . these are just words. A different level, if it's not too much trouble, yes?

LOGOVENKO (chuckling): If you wish . . .

146

(Some low noises like lilting whistles can be heard; someone's unclear exclamation and breaking glass)

LOGOVENKO: Apologies, I thought it was unbreakable.

(A pause of some ten seconds)

Is that the one?

GORBOVSKY: N-No . . . I think . . . No, it isn't. That one is over there, on the windowsill.

LOGOVENKO: Just a moment . . .

GORBOVSKY: No need to bother, you have convinced me. Thank you.

KOMOV: I do not understand what just happened. Was that a trick? I would—

(GAP IN THE RECORDING, 12 minutes and 23 seconds)

LOGOVENKO:—entirely different.

KOMOV: And what does fukamization have to do with it?

LOGOVENKO: Acceleration of the hypothalamus destroys the third impulse. We could not allow it until we learned how to restore it.

KOMOV: So you campaigned for the Amendment . . .

LOGOVENKO: Strictly speaking, you campaigned. But by our initiative, of course.

KOMOV: And Penguin syndrome?

LOGOVENKO: What?

KOMOV: Those phobias you induced with your experiments . . . Cosmophobia, xenophobia . . .

LOGOVENKO: Ah, I see, I see. Understand that there are several approaches and methods to discover the third impulse in a human. I prefer technical tools, but my colleagues—

KOMOV: So it was your doing?

LOGOVENKO: Of course! There are very few of us, we are creating our own race with our own hands, right now, as we go. I recognize it's possible that some of our methods may seem immoral, or even cruel, to you . . . but you have to admit that we never undertook any actions with irreversible consequences.

KOMOV: Let's assume so. If you disregard the whales.

LOGOVENKO: Excuse me. Not "let's assume," but we did not. As for the cetaceans—

(GAP IN THE RECORDING, 2 minutes and 12 seconds)

KOMOV:—wasn't our interest. Note, Leonid Andreievich, our people were on the wrong path but ended up being right in everything except their interpretation.

LOGOVENKO: Why "except"? I don't know who these people of yours are, but Maxim Kammerer uncovered us with complete precision. I haven't found out how he obtained the list of all ludens who were initiated in the last three years.

GORBOVSKY: Sorry, did you say "ludens"?

LOGOVENKO: We do not yet have a widely accepted name for ourselves. Most use the term *metahume*, as in beyond human. Some call themselves *misites*; I prefer to call us *ludens*. First, *luden* rhymes with *human*, second, one of the first ludens was Pavel Ludenov, our Adam. There's also the half-joking term *Homo ludens* . . .

KOMOV: Playing Man . . .

LOGOVENKO: Yes, Playing Man. And so, Maxim acquired a list of ludens and demonstrated it to me with great ingenuity, letting me know that we are no longer a secret to you. To be honest, I felt relieved. Finally there was a direct occasion to enter negotiations. I had felt someone's arm on my pulse for over a month, tried to carefully gauge what Maxim knew.

KOMOV: So you cannot read minds? Because the Readers—

(GAP IN THE RECORDING, 9 minutes and 44 seconds)

LOGOVENKO:—interfere. And that is not the only reason. We considered secrecy necessary mainly for your sake, for humanity's good. I would like you to be perfectly clear on this. We are not humans. We are ludens. Do not make that mistake. We are not the result of some biological revolution. We came into being because humanity has reached a certain level of socio-technological organization. Discovering the third impulse system in the human body would have been possible even a century ago, but initiating it only became a possibility in the first half of this century, while keeping a luden on the track of psychophysiological development, guiding him through all the levels to the end . . . that is, "raising a luden," in your terms, that is a very recent possibility.

GORBOVSKY: One moment, one moment! Does this mean that the third impulse is present in every human body after all?

LOGOVENKO: Unfortunately, no, Leonid Andreievich. That is the tragedy at hand. The third impulse is found at a rate not greater than one in a hundred thousand people. We do not yet know why and where it comes from. Most likely it is some ancient mutation.

KOMOV: One in a hundred thousand—that is still not such a small number, taking the billions of us . . . so this means schism?

LOGOVENKO: Yes. And therefore the secrecy. Please understand me, ninety percent of ludens have no interest in the fate of humanity, or in humanity in general. But there is also a group of those like me. We do not want to forget that we are flesh of your flesh and that we are of the same planet, so we have spent many years thinking about how to mitigate the consequences of this inevitable schism. Because it in fact looks like humanity is breaking up into a higher and lower race. What could be more repulsive than that? Of course, the analogy is superficial and essentially wrong, but you cannot avoid the feeling of humiliation at the thought that one of you has gone far past the limits that a hundred thousand can never reach. And the one who did can never escape the guilt. And by the way, the worst of it is that these fractures run through families, through friendships . . .

KOMOV: Does a metahume lose their former attachments?

LOGOVENKO: It is very individual. And not as simple as you imagine. A luden's attitude toward a human is, in most cases, like the attitude of a very experienced and highly preoccupied adult toward a cute but endlessly bothersome child. Then imagine the relationship between a luden and his father, luden and his best friend, luden and his teacher . . .

GORBOVSKY: Luden and his girlfriend . . .

LOGOVENKO: These are tragedies, Leonid Andreievich. Real tragedies.

KOMOV: I see that you take the situation to heart. Then maybe it's simplest to put an end to all this? After all, it's in your own hands . . .

LOGOVENKO: Does that not seem immoral to you?

KOMOV: Does it not seem immoral to you to put all of humanity into a state of shock? To burn low self-esteem into the mass consciousness, to present the finiteness of our children's abilities as a fait accompli?

LOGOVENKO: Thus I came to you, to look for a way out.

KOMOV: There is just one way out. You have to leave Earth.

LOGOVENKO: Excuse me, "you" as in who?

KOMOV: You, metahumes.

LOGOVENKO: Gennady Yurievich, I repeat again, the vast majority of ludens does not live on Earth. Their interests, their entire lives are away from Earth. You don't live in your bed, dammit! Only midwives like me and homopsychologists are constantly in touch with Earth . . . as are a few dozen of the most unhappy among us, those who cannot tear themselves away from friends and family!

GORBOVSKY: Ah!

LOGOVENKO: What did you say?

GORBOVSKY: Nothing, nothing, I'm all ears.

KOMOV: So you mean to say that the interests of metahumes and earthlings do not essentially overlap?

LOGOVENKO: Yes.

KOMOV: Is cooperation possible?

LOGOVENKO: In what area?

KOMOV: You would know better.

LOGOVENKO: I'm afraid you cannot be of use to us. As for ourselves . . . you know, there's an old joke. It sounds rather cruel under the present circumstances, but I'll mention it. You could teach a bear to ride a bicycle, but will the bear find it useful or fun? Please forgive me. But as you said, our interests do not overlap.

(Pause)

Of course, if the Earth and humanity were to be somehow threatened, we would come to your aid with all our might and no hesitation.

Komov: Thank you for that, at least.

(Long pause, sounds of bubbling liquid, clinking glass, swallowing, and coughing)

Gorbovsky: Well, well, this is a serious challenge to our optimism! But come to think of it, humanity has dealt with challenges worse than this . . . and I don't understand you at all, Gennady. You were so ardently advocating for vertical progress. Well, there you have it—vertical progress! In its purest form! Humanity spread out across blossoming plains under the clear blue sky, and then rushed upward! Sure, not the whole crowd, but why does it upset you so much? It's always been like this. And probably always will be. Humanity has always advanced into the future led by its best representatives. We've always felt pride in our geniuses, not disappointment in not being one of them. And Daniel Alexandrovich may be droning on here about being a luden and not human—that's all just terminology . . . You're human anyway; more than that, you're the people of Earth, and you won't get away from it. That's just foolhardy youth speaking.

Komov: You, Leonid Andreievich, sometimes simply amaze me with your frivolity! This is a schism! Schism, do you understand? And you are gushing some, forgive me, placid drivel!

Gorbovsky: Aren't you intense, my dear . . . Schism, yes, naturally. I wonder where you've ever seen progress with no schism? This is progress. In all its beauty. Where have you seen progress without shock, without sadness, without humiliation? Without those who advance far ahead and those who stay behind?

KOMOV: Oh, right! "And you who shall slay me, you I salute with hosanna and hymn!"

GORBOVSKY: It would be more fitting here with something like . . . hmm . . . "And you who shall surpass me, I see you off with hosanna and hymn!"

LOGOVENKO: Gennady Yurievich, please allow me to try to console you. We have good reason to believe that this will not be the last schism. In addition to the third impulse system in *Homo sapiens*, we have also discovered a fourth low frequency and a fifth, so far unnamed. We—even we—cannot guess what initiating these systems would result in. And we cannot guess how many more there are in humans . . . And what's more, Gennady Yurievich, a schism is already coming even among ourselves! It's inevitable. Artificial evolution is a cascading process.

(Pause)

Can't help it! After six scientific-technological revolutions, two technological counterrevolutions, and two gnoseological crises, you end up evolving, like it or not.

GORBOVSKY: Exactly. We could have quietly sat here like the Tagorans or the Leonidans, and we would have known no sorrow. But no, we had to go down the technology route!

KOMOV: Fine, fine. So what is a metahume, really? What are his goals, Daniel Alexandrovich? Motivations? Interests? Or is that secret?

LOGOVENKO: No secrets.

(The recording ends here; the remainder, 34 minutes and 11 seconds, has been irreversibly erased)

05/15/99; M. Kammerer

[END OF DOCUMENT 19]

✦✦✦

I'm ashamed to say it, but I had spent the last few days in a state of near euphoria. It felt as if unbearable physical stress suddenly disappeared. It must be what Sisyphus felt when the boulder finally tumbled down and he had the blissful opportunity to take a few breaths at the summit before starting it all over again.

Every earthling reacted differently to the Great Revelation. But by God, I had it worse than anyone else.

Rereading now all that I wrote above, I'm afraid that my feelings about the Great Revelation can be misunderstood. One could get the impression that I feared for humanity's fate then. Of course there were fears—I knew nothing about ludens then except that they existed. So there was fear. Just as there were short screams of *That's it, we're done for!* in my mind. And there was the sensation of a disastrously sharp turn, when the steering wheel is about to break out of your grasp and you're about to fly off somewhere, helpless like a savage in an earthquake . . . But above all that, there was the supremely humiliating awareness of my complete failure as a professional. We dropped the ball. Fumbled. Fell flat on our faces. Blew it, we bumbling amateurs . . .

And now all of that went away. Not, by the way, because Logovenko convinced me of anything at all, or made me believe him. No, it was completely different.

One and a half months was time enough for me to grow accustomed to the feeling of professional failure. (One of the small unpleasant discoveries you make with age is that the pangs of conscience can be silenced.)

The steering wheel was no longer breaking out of my grasp— I passed it to others. And now, with a measure of detachment, even, I remarked (to myself) that Komov is probably exaggerating, and Leonid Andreievich is, true to his nature, too convinced in the happy conclusion of any cataclysm . . .

I was finally in my own place, and with my usual concerns, such as organizing a constant and sufficiently intense stream of information for those who have to make the decisions.

On the evening of the fifteenth, I received Komov's orders to act as I saw fit.

On the morning of the sixteenth, I called in Toivo Glumov. With no prior explanation, I let him read the transcript of the conversation in Leonid's House. Remarkably, I was almost convinced of success.

What reason did I have to doubt it?

DOCUMENT 20

Date: May 16, '99

Participants: M. Kammerer, director of UE Department; T. Glumov, inspector

Subject: ***

Contents: ***

GLUMOV: What was in the gaps?

KAMMERER: Bravo. You have quite the self-control, kid. When I
finally figured out what was going on, I spent half an hour
running up the walls.

GLUMOV: So what was in the gaps?

KAMMERER: Nobody knows.

GLUMOV: How—What does that mean?

KAMMERER: Just that. Komov and Gorbovsky do not remember
what was in the gaps. They never noticed any gaps. And
restoring the recording is impossible. It's not even erased,
it's destroyed. The molecular structure of the recording lattice
in the gaps is gone.

GLUMOV: A strange way of negotiating.

KAMMERER: We will have to get used to it.

(Pause)

GLUMOV: So what will happen next?

KAMMERER: We don't know enough yet. Generally there are only
two possibilities. Either we learn to coexist with them, or we
do not learn.

GLUMOV: There is a third possibility.

KAMMERER: Don't be rash. There is no third possibility.

GLUMOV: There is a third possibility! They're not standing on
ceremony with us!

KAMMERER: That is not an argument.

GLUMOV: That is an argument! They didn't ask the World Council for permission! They have worked in secret for years to turn people into inhumans! They're conducting experiments on people! And even now, being discovered, they come to negotiations and dare—

KAMMERER (interrupting): What you want to propose can be done openly, making all of humanity witness to revolting violence, or in secret, despicably, behind society's backs—

GLUMOV (interrupting): Those are just words! The bottom line is that humanity must not be an incubator for inhumans, and certainly not a proving ground for their damned experiments! Sorry, Big Bug, you made a mistake. You should not have involved Komov or Gorbovsky. You put them in a stupid predicament. This is a COMCON-2 matter, entirely within our purview. I still think it's not too late. Let it be on our conscience.

KAMMERER: Listen, where do you get this xenophobia? These aren't Wanderers, these aren't the progressors you hate so much—

GLUMOV: I feel like they are even worse than progressors. They are traitors. Parasites. Like those wasps that lay eggs in caterpillars . . .

(Pause)

KAMMERER: Talk, talk. Speak your mind.

GLUMOV: I'm not saying more. It's pointless. Five years I've worked on this under you, and all five years I wobbled like a blind puppy . . . Tell me now at least, when did you find out the truth? When did you realize it's not the Wanderers? Six months ago? Eight months?

KAMMERER: Less than two.

GLUMOV: Still . . . A few weeks ago—I understand you had your own reasons, you didn't want to appraise me of all the details, but how could you hide from me that the very object had changed? How could you allow me to make a fool of myself?

Acting the fool in front of Gorbovsky and Komov . . . remembering that makes me sick!

KAMMERER: Can you suppose there was a reason for that?

GLUMOV: I can. Doesn't make it easier for me. I don't know the reason, can't even imagine it . . . and you don't look like you're about to tell me! No, Big Bug, I've had enough. I'm not fit to work with you. Let me go—I will leave anyway.

(Pause)

KAMMERER: I couldn't tell you the truth. At first I couldn't tell you the truth because I had no idea what we should do with it. Sidenote: I still don't know what to do with it, but the decisions are now in other hands . . .

GLUMOV: Don't justify yourself, Big Bug.

KAMMERER: Hush. You won't anger me anyway. You like the truth so much? You're about to get it. All of it.

(Pause)

Then I sent you off to the Oddball Institute and again had to wait—

GLUMOV (interrupting): What does the—

KAMMERER (interrupting): Quiet, I said! Telling the truth isn't easy, Toivo. Not just laying it all baldly out there, as young people love to, but presenting the truth to someone so . . . green, confident, all knowing, and all understanding . . . Be quiet and listen.

(Pause)

Then I got a response from the Institute. The response threw me off the rails. I had imagined I was just exercising routine caution, but it turned out . . . Look, you just read the transcript. Didn't you find something about it strange?

GLUMOV: It was all strange . . .

KAMMERER: Come on now, turn it on again. Read again, carefully, from the beginning, the header. Well?

GLUMOV: Only for Presidium members . . . What does that mean?

KAMMERER: Well? Well?

GLUMOV: You let me read an extremely classified document . . . Why?

KAMMERER (slowly and almost insinuatingly): As you noticed, the document has gaps. So I'm holding out the hope that, when your time comes, you will, for the sake of old memories and friendship, fill them in for me.

(Long pause)

That is the whole truth. As far as it concerns you. As soon as I found out that the Oddball Institute was sorting people, I sent all of you there, one after another, under various idiotic pretenses. It was basic caution, understand? To leave the opponent no opportunity. To be sure . . . no, I was sure anyway . . . to know with full certainty that all my employees are human.

(Pause)

They have a device there, supposedly for identifying oddballs. They put all the visitors through that device. What it really looks for is the so-called T wave mentogram, also known as the Logovenko impulse. If a person has a third impulse system suitable for initiation, the mentogram will show that accursed T wave. Well then, you have this wave.

(Long pause)

GLUMOV: That is nonsense, Big Bug.

(Pause)

You're being played for a fool!

(Pause)

It's a provocation! They want to take me out of the picture! I must have found out something important, though I don't understand what, and they want to be rid of me . . . It's obvious!

(Pause)

You've known me since I was a child! I've been through thousands of examinations, I'm a regular human being! Don't believe them, Big Bug! Who is your source? No, I'm not asking you for a name, just think, how does he know all that? He must himself be one of those . . . How can you believe him? (Shouting) It's nothing to do with me! I will leave anyway! But they will, in the same way, eliminate all of COMCON without firing a shot! Have you thought about that?

(Pause)

(In a resigned tone) What do I do now? Of course you know what I should do . . .

KAMMERER: Listen. No need to get so upset. Nothing has happened so far. Why are you shouting as if they "the knife already, grunting rapturously, swung"? After all, it's your decision! If you don't want it, everything will remain as it is!

GLUMOV: How do you know?

KAMMERER: I don't know anything. I know as much as you do. You just read the . . . This third impulse is just a potential—it has to be initiated. And only after that this transition from one level to another begins . . . I'd like to see them try it against your will!

(Pause)

GLUMOV: Yes. (Hysterical laughter) You gave me quite the scare, boss.

KAMMERER: You just didn't think it through.

GLUMOV: I will just run away! Let them try to find me! And if they do, if they pester me . . . you tell them that would be unwise!

KAMMERER: I don't think they will want to talk to me.

GLUMOV: How come?

KAMMERER: Well, see, we have no authority with them. We will have to get used to a completely new situation. We're not the ones choosing the time of conversations, or their topics . . . We've lost all control over events. And the situation itself is unprecedented! There is a power—and then some!—operating here on Earth, and we know nothing about it. Or rather, we only know what they allow us to, and that is almost worse than knowing nothing, I think you will agree. Uncomfortable, isn't it? No, I have nothing bad to say about these ludens, but we don't know anything good about them either!

(Pause)

They know everything about us, we know nothing about them. It's humiliating. Each and every one of us now feels humiliated when dealing with this situation . . . Now we will have to perform a deep mentoscopy on two World Council members, just to recover the historic conversation at Leonid's House. And, mind you, we don't want this mentoscopy, the World Council members don't want it, it humiliates us all, but we have no other way, even though the chances of success are quite problematic, as you understand . . .

GLUMOV: But we have our own people among them!

KAMMERER: Not among, but around. Among them is a dream. An unachievable one at that, I'm afraid. Who among them would want to help us? Why would they? What do they care about us? Huh? Toivo!

(Long pause)

GLUMOV: No, Maxim. I don't want to. I understand everything, but *I don't want to.*

KAMMERER: Afraid?

GLUMOV: I don't know. I just don't want that. I'm a human, and I don't want to be anything else. I don't want to look down on you. I don't want people I respect and love to seem like children. I understand that you hope part of me would remain human. Maybe you're even right to believe that. But I don't want to take the risk. I don't!

(Pause)

KAMMERER: Well . . . In the end, that is even commendable.

[END OF DOCUMENT 20]

✦ ✦ ✦

I was sure of success. I was wrong.

I didn't know you well enough in the end, Toivo Glumov, my boy. You seemed harder to me, more protected, more fanatical perhaps.

And finally, a few words about the real goal of this memoir of mine.

Readers familiar with the *Five Biographies of Our Age* have probably realized by now that my goal is to debunk the sensational hypothesis of P. Soroka and E. Brown, who claim that Toivo Glumov, back when he was a progressor in Arkanar, was noticed by the ludens and identified as one of their own. That he was, already then, transformed by them, taken to the appropriate level, and sent here to me, to COMCON-2, to act not even as a spy but as a disinformer, a misinterpreter.

That he spent the last five years encouraging all of COM-CON to hunt the Wanderers, interpreting every misstep, miscalculation, and oversight of the ludens as work of this hated supercivilization. He spent five years taking all of COMCON-2's leadership for a ride, and mainly, of course, his boss and mentor Maxim Kammerer. And when the ludens were finally exposed, he performed his last soul-wrenching theatrics and left the stage.

I think that any nonprejudiced reader who is unfamiliar with Soroka's and Brown's conjectures will, having reached these lines, shrug and think, What a load of nonsense, what a strange idea they have; it contradicts everything that I just read. As for the prejudiced reader, the reader who only knew Toivo Glumov from the *Five Biographies*, I have only one suggestion: try to consider the material presented here objectively; there is no need to spice up the luden question, which has by now become rather bland.

By all means, the history of the Great Revelation has a lot of blind spots, but I can with all responsibility state that they have nothing to do with Toivo Glumov. I also state with all responsibility that P. Soroka's and E. Brown's convoluted conjectures are simply careless drivel, another attempt to grab the left ear with the right arm by going over and under the left knee.

As for the "last soul-wrenching theatrics," I have only one regret, one I still curse myself for to this day. I didn't understand then, the old thick-skinned rhino that I was—I failed to sense that I was seeing Toivo Glumov for the last time.

DOCUMENT 21

From: Sverdlovsk, Topol 11, apt. 9716
To: M. Kammerer

Big Bug!
Logovenko paid me a visit today. We talked from 12:15 to 2:05 PM. Logovenko was very convincing. The main point: everything is not as simple as we imagine it. For example, it is claimed that the era of humanity's stationary development is coming to a close, and that an era of shocks (biosocial and psychosocial) is coming, and the main task of the ludens in relation to humanity is to act as guardians (like a catcher in the rye, so to speak). There are currently 432 ludens living and playing on Earth and in the cosmos. I have an offer to become the 433rd, and to do that I should go to Kharkov, the Oddball Institute, the day after tomorrow, May 20, at 10:00 AM.

The enemy of all humankind is whispering in my ear that only a complete idiot would refuse the opportunity to achieve superknowledge and power over the universe. I can silence that whispering with little effort, because I am an unassuming man, as you well know, and dislike elites in any forms. I will readily admit that our last conversation got much deeper under my skin than I would have liked. Feeling like a deserter is very unpleasant. I would not hesitate for a second to make that choice, but I am absolutely sure that once they turn me into a luden, there will be nothing (*nothing!*) human left in me. Admit it, you feel the same way deep down.

I will not go to Kharkov. I have spent these days thinking everything through, and I will not go to Kharkov because, first, it would be treason against Asya. Second, because I love my mother and hold her in the highest regard. Third, because I love my comrades and my own past. Becoming a luden would be my death. It is much worse than death, because I will be alive but unrecognizably repulsive to those who love me. An uppity, conceited, and arrogant type. And probably eternal as well.

Tomorrow I'm leaving for Pandora to be with Asya.

Farewell. I wish you luck.

Yours,

T. Glumov.

May 18, '99.

(END OF DOCUMENT 21)

DOCUMENT 22

COMCON-2, Ural-North.
Report 086/99
Date: November 14, '99
Author: Inspector S. Mtbevari
Subject: 081, "The Waves Extinguish the Wind"
Contents: Conversation with T. Glumov

In accordance with your instructions, I am reproducing from memory my conversation with former inspector T. Glumov that took place in mid-June of this year. Around 5:00 PM, when I was in my office, a videophone call came in, and T. Glumov's face appeared on the screen. He was happy, animated, and greeted me loudly. He had put on some weight since the last time I saw him. Approximately the following conversation took place.

> GLUMOV: Where did the boss disappear to? I've been trying to contact him all day, and no luck.
> ME: The boss is on assignment, he's not coming back anytime soon.
> GLUMOV: That's a real shame. I need him desperately. I would really like to speak to him.
> ME: Write a letter. It can be forwarded to him.
> GLUMOV (after some thought): It's a long story. (I remember this sentence exactly.)
> ME: Then tell me what to say to him. Or how to contact you. I'll write it down.
> GLUMOV: No, it has to be in person.

Nothing else of substance was said. Or, more precisely, nothing that I recall.

I would like to emphasize that, at the time, all I knew about T. Glumov was that he had quit for personal reasons and followed his wife to Pandora. For that reason I didn't think to undertake basic actions like registering the conversation, identifying the communication channel, notifying the president, etc. I can only add my impression that T. Glumov was in a room full of natural sunlight. At the time, he was presumably on Earth, in the Eastern Hemisphere.

Sandro Mtbevari

(END OF DOCUMENT 22)

DOCUMENT 23

To: President of the COMCON-2 Ural-North Sector
Date: January 23, '201
Author: M. Kammerer, director of UE Department.
Subject: 060, metahume T. Glumov

President!
I have nothing to report. The meeting did not place. I waited for him on Red Beach until dark. He never showed up.

Of course, it would have been possible to go to his home and wait for him there, but I think that would have been a tactical mistake. He is not trying to confound us. He simply forgets. Let's wait some more.

M. Kammerer

(END OF DOCUMENT 23)

DOCUMENT 24

To: COMCON-1, Chairman of the Metahume Committee G. Yu. Komov

My Captain!
I'm forwarding two curious texts that are directly related to your current passion.

TEXT 1: Note from T. Glumov to M. Kammerer
Dear Big Bug!
The fault is all mine. I'm ready to improve. In two days, on the second, I will *definitely* be at home at 8:00 PM sharp. I'll be waiting. Snacks are on me and I will explain everything. Although, as I understand it, there is no great need for that yet.

TEXT 2: Letter from A. Glumova to M. Kammerer, with T. Glumov's note attached
Dear Maxim!
He asked me to forward this note to you. Why didn't he send it to you directly? Why didn't he simply call you to arrange a meeting? I don't understand any of that. I rarely understand him at all as of late, even when we talk about apparently the simplest things. But I know that he is unhappy. As they all are. When he is with me, boredom consumes him. When he's out there, he misses me, or else he would not come back. Living like that is, of course, impossible, and he will have to choose. I know what his choice will be. He has been coming back less and less lately. I know some of his brethren have stopped coming back completely. There is nothing for them on Earth.

As for his invitation, I will of course be happy to see you, but don't expect him to come. I don't.
Yours,
A. Glumova

Naturally, Kammerer went to the meeting, and naturally T. Glumov did not show up.

They're leaving, Captain. Really, they have left. Completely. They left unhappy, as are those they left behind.

Humanity. This is serious.

It all is so unlike the apocalyptic visions we shared among ourselves four years ago! Remember how the old man Gorbovsky coughed with a sly smile, "The waves extinguish the wind . . ."? We all nodded in understanding, and you, I remember, even continued the quote with an expression meaningful to the point of cretinism. But did any of us understand him then? None of us did. And now, my captain, now that they have left and will never return, we all sighed in relief. Or in regret? I do not know. Do you?

Yours,

Athos

11/13/202

(END OF DOCUMENT 24)

THE LAST DOCUMENT

Maxim!

I cannot do anything. People bow to me in apology, assure me of their fullest respect and sympathy, but nothing changes. They have already turned Toivo into a "historical fact."

I understand why Toivo is silent—he doesn't care about any of this, and where is he, in what worlds does he walk?

I can guess why Asya is silent—the thought is unsettling, but they must have convinced her.

But why are you silent? You loved him, I know it, and he loved you!

M. Glumova

June 30, '226, Narva-Jõesuu

✦✦✦

As you see, Maya Toivovna, I am no longer silent. I have spoken. All that I could, all that I managed to say.

AFTERWORD

BY BORIS STRUGATSKY

This is the tenth, and last, work by Arkady and Boris Strugatsky in the Noon Universe series. We had planned another novel, though, under the working title *White Ferz* or *Operation Virus*, but never got around to even starting it. Curiously, the idea of that novel originated before *Waves*. Our diary for January 6, 1983, has this entry: "Thinking about a Maxim trilogy. Maxim infiltrates the Ocean Empire* to discover the fate of Tristan and Huron." And the very next day, January 7: "The Wanderers acting as progressors on Earth. Idea: Humanity, with its communist society, is dying in an evolutionary dead end. To continue, a synthesis with other races is needed." This is obviously the same idea out of which *Waves* came to be, though still very distorted and vague.

---

* TRANSLATOR'S NOTE: This refers to the Island Empire, the powerful seafaring nation on planet Saraksh featured in *The Inhabited Island*. The Island Empire name is used in most Strugatsky texts, but Boris Strugatsky referred to it as the Ocean Empire several times, so the translation retains this inconsistency.

Waves was written without anything unusual, let alone sensational, in the process. We started the draft on March 27, 1983, in Moscow, and finished the manuscript on May 27, 1984, likewise in Moscow. Throughout the entire period our excitement and creative appetite were fed by the goal of writing a documentary novel, ideally one composed of documents only, or at least of "documented" thought processes and events. This kind of writing was new to us, and it was interesting, as any novelty is. We greatly enjoyed coming up with the headers of report documents and the reports themselves, with their many intentionally dry, officious phrases and carefully thought-out numbers. The many names for witnesses of, analysts of, and participants in events were generated by a special program written for a powerful Hewlett-Packard calculator (we didn't yet have a computer); the first version of the "Instructions for the Fukamization of a Newborn" was quite professionally drafted by Arkady's friend Dr. Yuri Iosifovich Chernyakov.

As for the concept of Wanderer progressor activity on Earth, it didn't take us long to abandon it as the central plot point. It turned out to be much more interesting as a red herring, a feint, especially since we had long been interested in and attracted to the idea of humanity unwittingly and gradually giving birth to New Humans (*Homo super, Homo novus, Homo ludens*). The idea dates back to *Ugly Swans*, initially meant to be a meeting of border force lieutenant Victor Banev with the first superhumans—the clammies.

Finding a title proved unexpectedly challenging. Initially (in our letters and diary entries) we referred to the manuscript just as "Novel about Toivo." Then there was "Fait Accompli," in French for some reason, and only toward the end did the title "The Waves Extinguish the Wind" appear, and even then only as the subject line of report 086/99. We liked that title, and we decided to adopt it for the novel as a whole—quite a good title, really, calm and ambiguous, as a title should be.

The epigraph, on the other hand, caused some awkwardness. The aphorism was coined by Boris, personally and impromptu, in the middle of some polemics that I remember in detail to this day. He coined it and was amazed by his own imagination, because the phrase, it seemed to him, had a Gödelian depth and nontriviality to it. "To understand is to simplify"—what a phrase! Arkady also liked it, and we quickly decided to attribute the aphorism to our legendary writer Dmitry Strogov ("the Tolstoy of the twenty-first century") whom we had invented back in the '60s, and to make the attributed quote into an epigraph. But several years later, I discovered by complete accident that, as it turns out, those are words from a novel by Mikhail Ancharov—I think it was *Boxwood Forest*, or maybe *Soda-Sun*. Oh, that was quite a blow! That was a problem! We felt it would be a great shame to get rid of such a wonderful epigraph, and changing the attribution from Strogov, whom we had invented twenty years prior, to the very well-known Mikhail Ancharov just seemed silly. The novel had already been published, several times, with the original epigraph. So we decided to leave everything as it was. "I see no reason why a noble don (as in Dmitry Strogov) shouldn't, a century later, independently rediscover Ancharov's aphorism." Besides, B. Strugatsky did manage to do just that after, what was it, twenty years or so.

Waves turned out to be a concluding novel. All our characters had grown hopelessly old; all the problems once posed had been solved (or turned out to be unsolvable); we even explained to (thoughtful) readers who the Wanderers are and how they came into the universe, as our ludens are the Wanderers—or, rather, they are the Wanderer race that emerged out of Earth's civilization, the civilization of *Homo sapiens sapiens* (so great science names the subspecies that we all have the honor of representing). All that remained unwritten was one story meant for the Noon Universe—that of Maxim Kammerer reaching the very core of the terrible Ocean Empire.

Fans tell many legends about this unwritten novel. I've heard stories from people who know for sure that at least half the book was written, or that it was "given to the people" by the authors, or that a few have even held the manuscript … No, alas. The novel *was never written*; it was never even fully thought out. Here's its very general outline:

1. Prologue: Rotten Archipelago
2. Part 1: Coast
3. Part 2: Fields and Forests
4. Part 3: The Circle of Sun
5. Epilogue

The plot was to take place some short time after *The Beetle in the Anthill*—say, five years later—and long before the Great Revelation. The prologue was indeed developed in considerable detail. Boris could write it in several days (it's just ten pages), but he doesn't want to—that would be uninteresting as well as pointless. Part 1 is quite thought out; the major events are known but lack many, many significant details. For part 2, there's an overall outline with several known events. For part 3, a very general outline. Only one specific event is known from this part, the very last one (see the excerpt below from Boris's foreword to the collection *The Time of the Apprentices*).* As for the epilogue, it would have been some kind of concluding comment by perhaps Grisha Serosovin (or some other COMCONite) about everything up to that point, but not even very general notes exist here.

In his foreword to *The Time of the Apprentices*, Boris wrote something like the following . . .

✦✦✦

* TRANSLATOR'S NOTE: With Boris Strugatsky's permission, other authors wrote sequels to various Strugatsky books. A Russian-language collection of such sequels was published in 1996 as *The Time of the Apprentices*.

In the last Strugatsky brothers novel, thought out to a considerable degree and not written to any degree at all, a novel that even lacks a proper title (even a title we would have called "provisional" in a publishing application), a novel that will never be written because the Strugatsky brothers are no more and S. Vititsky* doesn't want to write it alone. This novel, then, had two ideas that attracted the authors.

First, we liked the world of the Island Empire, which seemed original and nontrivial, a world fashioned with the cruel rationality of a Demiurge who has given up on eliminating evil. This world was, roughly speaking, composed of three circles. The outer circle was the cloaca, the sewer, the hell of this world: all the dregs of society flowed there, all the addicts, ruffians, bastards, all the sadists and born killers, rapists, aggressive scum, perverts, beasts, moral cripples—the waste, pus, excrement of the whole society. Here, *they* rule; there are no punishments; life is governed by brute strength, turpitude, and hatred. This circle was the Empire's guard against the rest of the ecumene, its place from which to defend and to strike.

The middle circle was inhabited by regular people of no great excess, just like us. Some a bit better, some a bit worse—far from angels, but not devils either.

And in the center, there was the Just World. *Noon: 22nd Century.* A warm, welcoming, safe world of the soul, creativity and freedom, populated exclusively by talented, honorable, friendly people who fully adhere to all the highest rules of morality.

Everyone born in the Empire inevitably ends up in "his" circle; society would delicately (or rudely, if need be) push anyone to where he or she belonged based on talents, temperament, and moral potential. This pushing would be in part automatic and in part through a dedicated social mechanism (something like a moral police). This was a world where "to each his own" was

---

* TRANSLATOR'S NOTE: After Arkady Strugatsky's death in 1991, Boris Strugatsky used the pseudonym S. Vititsky for novels he wrote by himself.

the ruling principle in the widest interpretation possible. Hell, Purgatory, and Paradise. Classic.

Second, the authors liked the ending they imagined. In their mind, Maxim Kammerer would go through all the circles, reach the center, and be astonished at the heavenly life no worse than on Earth. As he's speaking to a high-ranking and highbrow local, trying to learn in detail how the Empire works, to reconcile the irreconcilable, to understand the unfathomable, Maxim hears a polite question: "Is your world not built like this?" And so he starts to speak, to explain, to expound all about the higher Theory of Upbringing, the teachers, the careful and meticulous work with every child's soul ... The local listens, smiles, nods, and remarks as if in passing, "Elegant. A very beautiful theory. But, sadly, completely impossible to implement in practice." And while Maxim is aghast, unable to speak, the local says the phrase for the sake of which the Strugatsky brothers wanted, until the very end, to write the novel after all. "The world cannot be organized the way you just explained to me," the local would say. "Such a world can only be imagined. I'm afraid, my friend, you live in a world that someone imagined, before you and without you, and you do not even suspect it."

The authors had intended for that phrase to be the very end of Maxim Kammerer's life story. It would have concluded the entire Noon Universe series. A summary of sorts for that entire worldview. Its epitaph. Or perhaps its verdict?

✦ ✦ ✦

Arkady and Boris were thinking about this novel during their last meeting, in Moscow in January 1991 ("01/18/91—Wrote letters. Discussing *Operation Virus* again"). I remember well that our discussions were slow, devoid of will or enthusiasm. It was an uneasy and uncomfortable time: Operation Desert Storm was getting underway in Iraq, the Alpha Group seized the TV tower in Vilnius,* the floodgates of the upcoming putsch were about to open, and so Maxim Kammerer's adventures in the Island Empire did not excite us at all—it was strange and even a bit obscene to be thinking them up. Arkady was feeling very sick, we were both nervous, we argued ... That was the final stretch, though of course neither of us knew or could even imagine ...

Why do I still sometimes think that someone will one day write this novel, or a very similar one? Not the Strugatsky brothers, of course. Not S. Vititsky. But who will?

---

* TRANSLATOR'S NOTE: After Estonia, Latvia, and Lithuania declared independence from the Soviet Union in 1990, there was a standoff between these three Baltic states and the Soviet government. In January 1991, Soviet forces, including the KGB-controlled Alpha Group, seized the TV tower in Lithuania's capital of Vilnius. The event marked a turning point in the conflict as Soviet troops fired on civilians, turning the political standoff into a violent crackdown.